PLAYING

Juliet

JOANNE STEWART WETZEL

Sky Pony Press

New York

Sky Pony Press books may be purchased in bulk at special discounts for sales promotion, corporate gifts, fund-raising, or educational purposes. Special editions can also be created to specifications. For details, contact the Special Sales Department, Sky Pony Press, 307 West 36th Street, 11th Floor, New York, NY 10018 or info@skyhorsepublishing.com.

Sky Pony® is a registered trademark of Skyhorse Publishing, Inc.®, a Delaware corporation.

Visit our website at www.skyponypress.com.

10 9 8 7 6 5 4 3 2 1

Library of Congress Cataloging-in-Publication Data is available on file.

Print ISBN: 978-1-63450-183-5
Ebook ISBN: 978-1-63450-929-9

Cover design by Sarah Brody
Cover image credit Thinkstock

Printed in the United States of America

For Jillian, Scott, and Graham,
who trod the boards

PROLOGUE

The actors are at hand and by their show
You shall know all that you are like to know.

Shakespeare's *A Midsummer Night's Dream*

There's a play by William Shakespeare that's so unlucky, no actor ever says the title out loud. They call it the Scottish play if they have to refer to it at all. For the past few weeks, two lines from that play have been running through my head, over and over again. To make it even worse, they're spoken by a witch:

By the pricking of my thumbs,
Something wicked this way comes

I shivered as I walked into the theater. Why did those lines keep coming back to me?

The lobby looked perfectly normal for six o'clock on a rainy Friday night. A trail of wet footprints led across the red tile floor. I followed their damp path, took a program for *Cinderella!* from the tottering stack on top of the ticket stand, opened it to the third page, and ran my finger slowly down the cast list. The actors and the roles they play were listed in order of appearance. I found my name about a quarter of the way down:

CAT.............BETH SONDQUIST

My biggest part yet. Twenty-eight lines and a solo! Suddenly, I felt fine. And I knew why those gloomy lines from Shakespeare had popped into my head—just part of my usual opening night jitters.

Cinderella! is my twelfth play. Not bad for someone who's twelve-and-a-half. One of these days I might even be able to call myself an actor.

I put the program in my backpack and glanced around casually to make sure no one else was in the lobby. Then I walked over to the back wall where a photograph was hanging slightly crooked against the redwood paneling. I straightened it and looked around one more time.

The only people in sight were the teenage couple in the picture, holding hands and gazing into each other's eyes.

They'd been staring like that for almost fifty years. A brass sign on the frame read:

Romeo and Juliet
First play
Oakfield Children's Theater

I touched the last word in the first line.

"Someday," I whispered, and headed for the dressing room.

Chapter One

Pins and poking-sticks of steel,
What maids lack from head to heel

Shakespeare's *The Winter's Tale*

This place is crawling with mice," whispered the back of the Horse.

I smiled in the darkness. Both the front and back of the Horse, six little Mice and I were all squeezed together in the left wing of the stage, waiting for our entrance.

The stage manager said, "Cue one, go!" softly into his headset. The audience lights dimmed as the opening music to *Cinderella!* began. The back of the Horse bent over and gripped the waist of the front of the Horse. Since only the front of the Horse gets to speak, they switch places for every performance. The tallest Mouse adjusted the saddle blanket covering the line where their costumes overlapped. And the smallest Mouse, Molly, clenched her hands into fists and stared down at the floor.

This was her first play.

All the Mice wear bright pink circles outlined in black on the end of their noses. When Molly was putting on her makeup, I saw her clean off that circle and redraw it at least four times. I leaned over to her and whispered, "Great nose," circling my finger over the tip of my own. She looked up, smiled, and took a step toward me.

"Break a leg," she said softly.

Before I could return with a "Break a leg" of my own, Molly raised her voice. "I remembered it's bad luck to say, 'Good luck.'"

"Shh! The audience can hear. We don't want anything to go wrong on opening night."

And as soon as I said it, I realized that something was already wrong.

"You're standing on my tail!" I whispered, pointing frantically to where my fluffy fur tail was trapped under her black ballet slipper. In the dim backstage light, she couldn't see what the problem was.

"You're standing on my tail!" I whispered even louder.

A surge of music drowned out my voice.

Molly stepped closer to hear what I was trying to tell her. Her other foot landed on my tail just as I tried to pantomime the problem by giving it a little jerk. The music paused and we both heard the rip as the tail came off in my hand.

"Beth, what are you going to do?" Molly sounded terrified.

"Don't worry," I said, patting her shoulder. "The stage manager always has safety pins for costume emergencies."

I managed not to step on anyone else's tail as I backed out of the crowd of animals and headed for the dim blue light on Austin's desk.

Austin Santiago, the stage manager, was dressed in black, like all the crew members. He sat hunched over a copy of the script, talking softly into his headset, his dark hair sticking straight up as if it were standing at attention.

I waved my tail in front of him until I got his attention and mouthed, "Emergency repair."

"What are you doing here?" Austin asked. "Actors are supposed to stay in the dressing room until it's time for their entrance."

Busted! Now there was no way I could finish watching this play from the wings. Austin would be on the lookout for me. He ran a tight backstage. Austin's only fourteen, which is young to be a stage manager, even at our theater, but he's really good at his job.

He picked up a battered black box from his desk, shook it, frowned, then looked into it.

"Empty?" he said. "I thought I checked last night." He looked into it again. "Not a single pin."

"I'll run down to the costume shop and bring some back."

Austin nodded and turned his attention to an urgent voice speaking through his headset. I left him to deal with his next emergency, glancing at the clock on his desk as I left. I only had fifteen minutes until my entrance.

"Emergency repair," I called as I entered the costume shop.

No one was there.

Our costume mistress, Mrs. Lester, was probably in the rack room. I stepped around the huge cutting table that ran down the middle of the room, opened the door, poked my head in, and called again. "Emergency repair!"

No one. Just thousands of costumes hanging silently on the racks.

Where was she? I ran over to the cutting table and grabbed the safety pin box.

Empty.

I looked on the table, on the floor. Not a safety pin to be seen. I glanced up at the monitor. The opening music was still playing. I had a little time left.

Actors don't fix their own costumes when the play is running, but I was out of options. Thank goodness I was wearing a leotard underneath. I stepped out of my black fur suit and headed for the line of sewing machines that sat against the rear wall.

I turned my costume inside out and slid the tail between the thick fabric. I locked it in place under the needle, sewed the tail and the ripped seam together with a careful line of stitches, reversed, and sewed back over it.

Stacks of boxes stretched from floor to ceiling on the wall to my right. I glanced at the labels on the top row. ANGEL WINGS, COWBOY HATS, FAUN EARS, TURBANS. I looked away quickly. Usually when I work down here, I try to make up a play that includes all the items stored on one shelf, but I had no time to waste.

I reversed once more and sewed another line. That should keep it together practically forever, I thought.

I pulled the cat suit out of the machine and started to turn it right-side out. That was when I realized that the tail was on the inside.

I'd sewn it in backwards.

Three times.

To keep it together practically forever.

I glanced up at the monitor that showed the stage. The performance had started. I had less than ten minutes until my entrance. I grabbed a pair of scissors and started to pick out the stitches. I was still tugging at the stubborn threads when the door to the shop opened.

Relief flooded through me as Mrs. Lester appeared, carrying a large bolt of red felt. As always, her graying blonde hair was escaping from her ponytail and six or seven straight pins were stuck haphazardly in the front of her sweater.

She started when she saw me sitting there in my tights and dumped the felt on the cutting table.

"Beth!" she exclaimed. "Shouldn't you be onstage?"

"I need help," I said and held up the mess I'd made.

She took one look, picked up the pair of scissors I'd put down, and cut off the tail. Then she pulled a threaded needle from her sweater and started sewing. She paused for a moment to glance up at the monitor showing the stage.

I did, too. About six minutes left.

"Why on Earth didn't you pin it?" she asked.

"All the safety pins are missing," I said. "The stage manager doesn't have any, and I couldn't find a single one down here."

Mrs. Lester shook her head but kept on stitching. "I've had so much on my mind. I must have forgotten to order new ones. Check the pincushion on the right-hand side of my desk. I think there's enough there for the stage manager."

I hurried over to her tiny office. It was crammed as full as the rest of the shop, but I saw what I needed immediately. A giant red pincushion, dangling a long chain of safety pins, sat on a magazine in the middle of her desk.

As I picked it up, I glanced down at the page it held open. Big black lettering across the top screamed EMPLOYMENT. About five ads, all for a costume mistress, were heavily circled in red. Two had stars drawn next to them.

I was staring so hard, I didn't realize Mrs. Lester had come in the room until I heard a sharp intake of breath. She reached over my shoulder, grabbed the magazine, and held it behind her back as she handed me my mended costume.

By the time I'd zipped it up, the magazine had disappeared and Mrs. Lester was looking at me anxiously.

"I don't want you to worry," she said. "No matter what you've heard."

I didn't say anything. I couldn't. I didn't know what she was talking about.

My silence must have worried Mrs. Lester because she leaned toward me and kept speaking, obviously trying to reassure me. "This theater is not going to close."

"Close?" I could barely say the word. Those lines from the Scottish play were running through my head again.

By the pricking of my thumbs . . .

Mrs. Lester looked at me sharply. "You haven't heard that the theater is closing?"

I shook my head and tried to speak, but she wouldn't let me.

"It's only a rumor, nothing to worry about. I won't say anything else. Don't ask me about it." And she glanced up at the monitor and said the only thing guaranteed to stop me from asking any more questions: "If you don't leave right now, you're going to miss your entrance."

CHAPTER TWO

Here is that
which will give language to you, cat: open
your mouth; this will shake your shaking

Shakespeare's *The Tempest*

I stared at her for a moment in bewilderment, then grabbed the pins and ran up the stairs. I couldn't stop to think about what I'd just heard.

Sometimes people outside the theater say, "The show must go on!" like it's some kind of joke. It isn't. It's the most important thing of all. I had to become a cat and make people laugh before I could think.

Or panic.

The music for the Frog's dance was just ending as I reached the wings. Austin gave me a thumbs-up sign when

I dropped the pins on his desk, then started to cue the lights for my entrance.

I walked over to the curtains masking the side of the stage, took a deep breath, and exhaled slowly, clearing my mind of everything that had just happened. *Cat*, I thought as I waited for the applause for the Frog to die down. As Cat, I could do things I'd never be able to do in real life. *Cat*.

I sauntered slowly onstage into the glare of the lights, swinging my tail, and said my first lines as though nothing had happened: "Here Parmesan, here Mozzarella, here Cheddar!

Come out little mice. Let's play Lunch.

You can be It."

While I'm upstage trying to catch a Mouse, Cinderella is downstage, being kind to an ugly Old Hag who's really her fairy godmother in disguise. My best friend, Zandy Russell, is the Old Hag. She's got a great voice, so she gets all the big parts—like the Fairy Godmother—that call for someone who can really sing.

The script calls for us to exit at the same time. Zandy leaves by climbing down one of the trap doors in the floor of the stage. To the audience, it looks like she's disappearing magically because her exit is covered by a big cloud of violet smoke.

When the technical rehearsal began and all the special effects rolled out, I realized the Cat was running offstage because she was scared silly by that big purple cloud. So

I showed her fear. The director liked what I was doing so much she encouraged me to work up the action even more. Now I'm onstage alone for almost a full minute after Zandy leaves. Tonight was the first real test of how well I could act without lines.

The audience started laughing when I jumped in fright at the smoke, kept laughing as I tried to run away from it, then started to clap, still laughing, as I slowly slunk off the stage.

That applause was just for me.

The prop master was standing in the wings, waiting to hand Cinderella a tray stacked with dirty dishes. He held his thumb up and grinned.

"Cin-der-elllll-a," the Stepmother called from the wings. But the laughter was still so loud she had to wait and call again.

I stopped to listen until the laughter died down.

Emily Chang, who plays Cinderella, came offstage in answer to the Stepmother's call. She leaned over and whispered, "Good job," before she picked up a tray from the props table and went back on. On the other side of the stage, Austin gave me a small salute from the stage manager's desk.

I floated all the way to the dressing room.

I opened the door and took a deep whiff of the familiar odor: makeup and old socks. It smelled wonderful.

Zandy sat at one end of the makeup table that ran the length of the room. She waved at my reflection in the mirror, pointed at the chair next to her, and went back to tucking her dark brown hair under a headband. No matter how big a part she's had, Zandy's always been my best friend.

The two high school girls who play the Ugly Stepsisters, Pam Thompson and Tina Peers, were doing their homework at the other end of the table. Pam wore a lime green dress, a purple wig, and a huge fake nose. Tina was in shocking pink with blue hair. She reached up and scratched her nose carefully around the big wart, which matched the color of her wig.

I shook my head in sympathy as I watched them.

All that homework!

I wasn't looking forward to high school. I hated to think of doing math problems in the dressing room whenever I was offstage.

And then I remembered . . . that rumor Mrs. Lester had talked about. If it was true, our theater could be closed by the time I was in high school. I shook my head again to clear away that ridiculous thought. The Oakfield Children's Theater couldn't close. It had been here forever. Though why would Mrs. Lester be looking for a new job if the theater wasn't closing?

By the pricking of my thumbs . . .

This time I knew the lines from the Scottish play had nothing to do with stage fright. Something wicked was threatening my theater. I needed to talk to Zandy.

"I beat you back, E-lizzy-beth," she said as I sat down beside her.

She dug a big white glop out of a jar of cold cream. As she smeared it on her face, the wrinkle lines of her Old Hag makeup melted into gray circles. She picked up a tissue and began wiping the goop off one cheek.

Some of the little Mice were playing a game under the costume racks. The last thing I wanted was for one of them to overhear me and start to worry. So I leaned over close to Zandy, but even then I couldn't bring myself to put what I'd heard into words.

Zandy had gone through three tissues before I spoke.

"Mrs. Lester's looking for a new job," I said softly.

"Rats." She finished mopping the last bit of cold cream off her face. "We'll miss her."

She wet a sponge and smoothed the base for her Fairy Godmother makeup on her right cheek.

"Zandy . . ." I glanced at my reflection and broke off. The painted whiskers on my cheeks wiggled earnestly every time I spoke. A strand of my hair had escaped, its light blonde color standing out against the black fur of the Cat's headdress. I tucked it back in and realized Zandy was staring at my face in the mirror, too.

"What's the matter?" she asked.

"Mrs. Lester . . ." The rest came out in a rush. "She said there was a rumor the theater is going to close."

Zandy was so startled she raised her voice. "Close? The Oakfield Children's Theater?"

The Ugly Stepsisters looked up from their books simultaneously. Pam, the one in the purple wig and fake nose, turned to Tina. "How did they find out?" she asked.

At least, I think that's what Pam said. She'd dropped her voice really low. If there's anything you learn by spending all your time at the theater, it's how to control your voice.

Tina shook her blue ringlets. "*Pas devant les enfants.*"

And they both shut their books, got up, and left the dressing room.

I looked up at the TV monitor that showed the stage and frowned. "Isn't it too early for their entrance?"

Zandy gave the monitor a quick glance, then turned back to the mirror. "Way too early." Now she was frowning, too. "You know my mom's made me take French since I was about three?" She whispered so quietly I had to watch her lips moving to understand her.

I nodded at her mirror image. Of course I know. If there's a class around, Zandy's mom has signed her up for it.

Zandy picked up a false eyelash with two-inch-long silver lashes and bobbed her head ever so slightly at where the Ugly Stepsisters had sat. "Tina said, 'Don't talk in front of the kids.' My mother used to say that a lot when I was little. Before we moved to Oakfield."

She paused. Zandy doesn't talk much about her life before she moved here.

"Whenever I hear it, I always think something really horrible is going to happen," she finally continued.

I picked up the lid to the jar of cold cream and screwed it back on. "We could ask Tina or Pam. They definitely know something."

Zandy knew she'd be the one doing the asking. She opened her mouth as wide as she could and stuck the eyelash on her right eyelid. She batted her eyes to see if it was on tight. "Why not just ask Mrs. Lester?"

"She told me not to ask her anything else. She sounded like she meant it."

"Pam, then," Zandy said decisively, reaching for the second eyelash. "I've been in a couple of plays with her. She's really nice."

Zandy's been in a couple of plays with almost everyone. Her first audition was on the day after her seventh birthday, the first time she was old enough to try out. She got cast as the youngest daughter in *The Sound of Music*. With a solo. She's been cast in almost every production she's tried out for ever since.

That was my first audition, too. I didn't even get a callback.

Zandy glued on the second silver strip and batted her eyes again. "I hate the way these feel," she said and slipped off the headband protecting her hair.

The Mice started to get up and head for the door. I checked the monitor and stood, too.

"We'll catch Pam during intermission," I whispered and left for my next entrance.

But Pam wouldn't be caught. We couldn't find her—or Tina—anywhere.

"They can't duck us when the play's over," I said. "If we don't run into them in the lobby, we'll catch them when they're changing."

After the play, the lobby was so packed with the actors and the audience all talking and gesturing and hugging, it was almost impossible to move. I could see my dad on the far side of the room next to the light switch. That's where my parents always wait for me. My dad's really tall and blond, so he's easy to spot. I plunged into the crowd only to be stopped by one of my little brother's peskiest friends.

"Beth, could you sign my program for me?" he asked.

He looked at me almost shyly as he handed me a pen. "The Cat was really funny," he said as I wrote my name. Then two kids from my class came up. And suddenly it seemed as if everybody in the lobby wanted my autograph.

It feels really good to have perfect strangers tell you what a great job you did. It feels even better when some of them say you're a really talented actress. It took a while to work my way across the room to my parents, but I didn't mind.

I was almost there when the ninth person stopped me. I waved at my parents before I signed her program. Mom waved back enthusiastically. She's not as tall as my dad, but she stands out in a room almost as much because she's got all this energy. She moves her arms when she talks and her face always shows exactly what she's thinking. My little brother, R. J., has her brown hair. I got my dad's. I could see my dad and R. J. out of the corner of my eye, leaning against the wall with their arms crossed, obviously ready to go home.

My parents were congratulating Zandy when I finally reached them. Mom handed me a bouquet of red and white carnations and gave me a quick hug. "What a performance! But it looks like everyone's told you that already. How many people asked you to sign their programs?"

Zandy and I both shrugged, as though we hadn't been counting, but I was grinning as I handed the flowers back. "Hold these while I change?"

"I always do."

Dad leaned down for his hug. "Good job." He held me at an arm's length to look at my face. "Great whiskers! Any chance you two could change quickly? I've had a rough day."

Poor Dad. He was usually in bed by nine o'clock.

"Ten minutes," I promised, and we headed off to intercept the Ugly Stepsisters.

Pam and Tina must have made one of the fastest costume changes on record. They were heading out of the dressing room just as we got there.

Zandy put her hands on her hips as we watched the door close behind them.

"Something really *is* going on."

"I've felt something was wrong for weeks," I said. "You know that line from Shakespeare: 'By the pricking of my thumbs . . .'" I clapped my hand over my mouth, dumbfounded by what I'd done.

"I don't know Shakespeare," Zandy said, starting to unzip her Fairy Godmother costume. "You're the literary one. I only do musicals."

I felt as if someone was staring at me behind my back. I turned around slowly to see Emily Chang holding Cinderella's ball gown in one hand and a hanger in the other, looking at me in disbelief. She walked over and bent down to speak almost in my ear.

"Do you realize you just quoted the Scottish play?" she asked urgently, but so quietly only I could hear her. "That's the worst thing you can do in a theater."

Mrs. Macintosh is our director. At the beginning of every play, she tells us to come see her if anything is bothering us. The last thing she says is, "My door is always open."

I went to talk to her as soon as I changed. I'd never gone by myself to see Mrs. Mac before, but Zandy had to take her crown and wand down to the costume shop and I was too worried to wait. I may not have been cast in the first play I tried out for, but I was part of this theater now, and I wasn't about to let it close. I had worked too hard to get here.

I hurried down the hallway to Mrs. Mac's office, but I stopped when I reached her door.

It was closed.

I stood and stared at it for a minute, the quote from the Scottish play running through my head as if it were printed right above the doorknob.

Thank goodness Zandy always sleeps over on opening night. I needed to talk to her so badly. I turned around and headed back to the lobby.

The crowd had thinned out but I couldn't see Zandy anywhere. My dad broke the news to me: "Zandy had to go home, Scooter. Her mom came to pick her up. They asked us to tell you she can't sleep over tonight."

R. J. always plays with plastic monsters in the car. I buried my face in the spicy scent of the carnations from my parents and listened to him grunt and moan next to me as he knocked his monsters together in battle. The car turned left and in the backseat, R. J. and I swayed with the motion. But not Zandy.

There had to be a major emergency for her to go home without waiting to tell me why. Zan has super perfect manners. Now I had to worry about her as well as whether our theater was closing.

I looked out the car window. The rain had finally stopped. Big houses on big lawns changed to medium houses on medium lawns. The fruit trees were in bloom, and the white flowers on the plum trees looked like tufts of popcorn whenever the car's lights shone on them.

I suddenly became aware of what R. J. was playing.

"Save the Cat," he said, and a green Tyrannosaurus rex was knocked to the seat between us by a handful of action heroes.

"Am I the Cat?" I asked.

His action figures answered in as gruff a voice as an eight-year-old can manage. "You are the Cat. We save you from monsters."

"When I was in *A Christmas Carol*, you guys attacked me." I've spent a lot of years talking to action figures.

"The Cratchett girl wasn't funny. The Cat is funny."

Action figures talk in very short sentences.

My parents were talking about gardening. Right now they were debating the best fertilizer for their roses. I stopped listening and started reliving my conversation with Mrs. Lester. My dad had to call my name twice before I realized he was speaking to me.

"Beth, you won't believe this, but some guy sitting in the row behind us said you should be doing professional work. On TV, no less."

"Was he a TV producer?" I asked. "Or an agent?"

Both my parents laughed. I stroked the soft gray velvet of the upholstery with my index finger, counting the seconds while I waited for the reply.

One. Two. Three. Four.

Dad made another left turn before he answered.

Five. Six. Seven.

"I don't know who he was. But I told him straight out, 'My daughter just does this for fun. She wants to be a lawyer.'"

"Just like her dad," Mom chimed in.

I didn't say anything. I never do. There are some dreams you don't put into words. And it was my own fault my parents thought I wanted to be a lawyer.

Eight's my lucky number. I didn't reach it.

I stared out the window at the medium-sized houses we were passing. Dark. Lights on. Lights on. Dark. Dark. Dark.

What would I do if my theater went dark forever?

Chapter Three

Now must we to her window,
And give some evening music to her ear.

Shakespeare's *Two Gentlemen of Verona*

The answering machine was blinking as we walked in
the house.

"Hey, E-lizzy-beth," said Zandy. "Sorry I couldn't come
over." Her words slowed down. "I'd really, really love to see
you tonight, but . . ."

Really, really. I froze when I heard the words and waited
for her to say when.

Tonight. Followed by *but.* Perfectly clear.

Zandy's voice grew brisk again. "Meet me at 12:30
tomorrow after my tennis lesson? Talk to you soon."

My parents were still bustling around the room. They'd heard the message at the same time I did, but they didn't have a clue what Zandy had just asked me to do. It looked like our emergency plan was going to work.

I turned my pillow over in frustration. I could not let myself fall asleep. I rolled over on my back and stared up at the ceiling, fighting to keep my eyelids from closing. Then a sliver of light shone through a gap in the doorway, and I looked up to see my door opening slowly.

"Still awake?" My mom sat down on the bed. "I thought you might be missing Zandy."

I sat up and poked a hand out of the covers. She stroked it softly with her fingertips.

"Big day," she said.

"Mmmm," I agreed. I felt so peaceful, like I was a little kid again.

"You looked like you were having fun onstage tonight."

"Mmmm." If I didn't watch it, I'd fall asleep after all.

"I'm happy to hear that. I worry about how much fun you miss."

"I don't miss anything," I said sleepily.

"You missed Amanda's birthday party last week."

Well, of course I did. "I had rehearsal," I said, but Mom went on like she didn't hear me.

"You missed Kim's party last month."

"I had auditions."

"It sounds like a disease," Mom said. "And the results are the same. You're missing so many things other kids get to do. You had to drop swim team last summer."

"I got a really good part."

She pulled the comforter up over my arms and patted it in place before she reached over and stroked my cheek. Her hand lay there softly as she asked, "Do you think you spend too much time at the theater?"

I actually felt my mouth fall open in surprise. What a question for my own mother to ask. I was five years old when I saw my first play. I haven't wanted to be anywhere but in a theater ever since.

It wasn't easy for me to get into acting, not like Zandy. It took more than a year of tryouts until I finally got cast in *Alice in Wonderland*. I think Zandy was as happy as I was when I got my first part, even though I had no lines. I was just one of the playing cards, but I learned a lot as the Eight of Hearts. By the end of the play, I had become a theater kid, one of the family. How could my mother think I spent too much time at the theater?

"There's no place else I want to be," I said firmly and shivered, despite the warmth of the comforter.

I waited thirty minutes after my mother left my room before I climbed out the window. The nice thing about living in a one-story house is that climbing out the window's about as hard as climbing out of a bathtub. In two minutes I had grabbed my bike from beside the house and was on my way. It's only a ten-minute ride to Zandy's, but in the dark it's hard to see the road, so I was glad there was a full moon.

I wore my bike helmet, because I didn't want to give anyone a reason to stop me, and heavy denim jeans, because Zandy's room is on the second floor.

She was looking for me as I rode up.

She threw down a pair of leather gloves, and I put them on before I climbed up the rose trellis beneath her window. I only got stuck on the thorns twice. The gloves and my jeans kept me from getting seriously scratched. I've only done this once before. Zandy's never tried it.

"What happened?" I said as I climbed over the windowsill.

"Shh," she whispered and pointed at the wall next to her bed.

The first time I snuck over, Zandy's mom heard us talking and came to investigate. Fortunately their house has hardwood floors and we heard her footsteps creaking down the hall toward us. I was under the bed long before she reached us, but Zandy panicked and her mom opened the door to see her standing next to the bed by her nightstand.

"I was just talking to Beth," Zandy had said. Her voice sounded like she was confessing to robbing a bank.

Her mom had looked past her to the phone on the nightstand and said, "I'll have to take your phone away if you don't stop calling so late at night. You could wake Beth's parents."

And that was that.

But we didn't want to risk another close call, so we figured out how to talk without making any noise.

It was time to try it. We got into position before we said anything else. Zandy lay in bed under the covers, and I sat on the floor next to her head so we could whisper right into each other's ear—and I could roll under the bed if we heard any footsteps approaching.

This time Zandy spoke first. "Sorry I couldn't sleep over. My dad called."

"Is anything wrong?" Zandy and I slept at each other's house so often, I knew her dad's phone schedule as well as she did: 8:00 a.m. on the first Saturday of every month. Since he works in Saudi Arabia, there's a huge time difference. I'd never known him to call her at night.

"He's coming to visit next week."

I reached up and grabbed her hand and started shaking it like she'd just won a boxing match. "Awesome! When?"

"He gets in Sunday."

"Tomorrow?"

"Yeah." Zandy dropped my hand and turned onto her back.

The moonlight made the room so bright I could see her fingers moving as she started twirling a lock of hair. I sat there, watching, as the twirling became faster and faster.

"How long has it been since you've seen him?" I finally asked.

"Two years and five months."

The mattress shook as Zandy rolled over. "I wish I had your parents," she whispered fiercely.

"They're not perfect."

"They don't hate each other. They love you. If you're a Child-Of-Divorce it's different." Zandy was talking like it was funny, but I knew she was deadly serious. "Half the time your parents care more about hurting each other than about what's important to you. You never know if they love you or just want to use you as another way to get even with each other."

"Your mom loves you." I knew that.

"Partly," said Zandy. "Partly she hates my dad."

I stared at the moonlit shadows cast by the big tree outside her window. The wind must have picked up. The branches were swaying on the wall.

I couldn't imagine not seeing my dad every day—not hearing him call me Scooter.

"What are you and your dad going to do when he gets here?" I asked.

"Oh, Beth, I don't know," she whispered. "I only saw him once or twice a year before he moved to Saudi Arabia and we never had anything to talk about then. I never know what to say to him when he calls."

She started to twirl her hair again.

"*Cinderella!*'s still running next week," I said. "Take him to see you as the Fairy Godmother. He'll be so impressed by your singing, that's all he'll want to talk about."

The twirling stopped. "Would that be okay? We wouldn't really be spending the time together. He'd just be watching me."

"Your mom just watches. My parents just watch. It's what parents do."

"That would be so perfect," Zandy said. Even though she was still whispering, I could hear the excitement in her voice. And then she added in the most despairing tone, "What if it's sold out for next week?"

"Tell Mrs. Mac. She'll get him in somehow, even if he has to usher."

Zandy giggled softly. "It could work," she said. "But what if . . ." She answered her own question. "Even if the theater is going to close, it won't happen by next week."

"Yeah." This time I was the one sounding sad.

"What did Mrs. Mac tell you?"

I squirmed uncomfortably on the floor. "Nothing."

"You did go see her, right?"

"Yes." Thank goodness I could at least say that. "But her door was closed."

"Closed?"

We both sat in silence for a long moment.

"Wow," said Zandy. She reached down and squeezed my shoulder. "We'll both go see Mrs. Mac tomorrow and ask her what's going on." She started counting off her morning on her fingers. "Eight o'clock, Dad. Nine-thirty, vocal lesson. Eleven o'clock, tennis. Can you meet me at twelve-thirty in the lobby?"

"Sure."

I could feel the tension drain out of my body. Zandy had taken charge. She was so good at getting things done. She'd talk to Mrs. Mac and find out what was making everyone so jumpy.

But something she'd said . . .

"Eight o'clock, Dad?" I asked.

"My father didn't know his schedule so he's going to phone again in the morning." Zandy said. "I'll ask him to go to *Cinderella!* then."

She rolled over on her back once more and the twirling began again, but this time slower, more peacefully.

When you're sitting in the dark and you can't see who you're talking to, you can say things you'd never say otherwise.

"My mother said I spend too much time at the theater." My voice broke slightly.

There was a long silence as the twirling grew faster. Finally she let out a sigh. "I don't know what you'd do if it closed."

"You'd miss it as much as I would."

"I've got my voice lessons. I could still sing at recitals and stuff." Zandy leaned over the edge of the bed. "Have you told your parents you want to be an actor when you grow up?"

No, I'd never said that.

Ever.

Except to myself and to the photograph of Juliet hanging on the wall of the lobby.

I started to once. In third grade, Mrs. Warren asked the whole class what we wanted to be when we grew up. I knew I wanted to be an actor, but I'd never even gotten a callback. So I searched my brain frantically. What other jobs were there?

"Maybe an archeologist," I said. "Or a lawyer, like my dad."

A friend of my mother's was volunteering in my classroom that day. As soon as she got home, she called my mom to tell her about the "charming" thing I'd said in class.

No one ever mentioned archeology to me. But boy, did I hear about becoming a lawyer. My dad beamed at me all through dinner that night. I couldn't tell him I only said I wanted to be a lawyer so no one would laugh at me. I figured he'd forget about it in a few weeks. Not my dad.

I know he thinks his work is exciting, but when he talks about it, it sounds like he's always working with really unhappy people. I don't want to do that all my life. But if

I told him the truth, he'd be hurt and disappointed. So I've never said anything.

How could Zandy ask me if I'd told my parents?

"I've got to go."

I started to get up but Zandy reached out a hand and pushed me back down. "No one at the theater ever talks about becoming an actor because it's so hard to make it," she whispered. "I know we're supposed to be doing theater just for fun. But we all know there are a few kids who could go on and become professionals. Like Emily Chang."

I nodded and leaned back against the wall. Emily was not only a good actress—she was a triple threat: she sang and danced, too.

"You know people are starting to talk about you," Zandy continued.

Even with a full moon, there wasn't enough light in the room for Zandy to see how deeply I was blushing.

"Your parents can't help you if they don't know what you want." Zandy sounded worried.

"They're not that thrilled about me acting right now. If I told them I wanted to become a professional, they'd go ballistic."

"No," she said, shaking her head. I could feel the bed move with total conviction. "If they knew you really wanted it, they'd help you."

I was smiling when I climbed out of Zandy's window. She always made me feel better.

That smile would have lasted all the way home if I'd remembered to put the leather gloves back on. When I reached for the first bar of the trellis, I grabbed the rose vine growing behind it, hard, and pushed a thorn deep into my thumb. I couldn't cry out, but the pain was so sharp, my thumb throbbed all the way home.

CHAPTER FOUR

Wilt thou spit all thyself?

Shakespeare's *Pericles*

I overslept Saturday morning, but I joined my family at the kitchen table before I biked over to the theater. My parents won't let me out of the house if I don't eat first.

"Tuna fish sandwiches for breakfast? Interesting choice," I said politely as I sat down.

"Some people eat *lunch* at noon." My mother looked up from her newspaper and glanced at the clock. "But you're welcome to fix yourself something else."

"Tuna's SEE FOOD," said R. J., opening his mouth to reveal a half-chewed glob.

I decided to have the tuna anyway.

Mom was talking half to my dad and half to the newspaper, so I was mostly concentrating on peeling the crusts off my bread when I heard her gasp. Mom is a very noisy newspaper reader but this was loud even for her.

"Did you see how much that house on Brighton Street sold for? The one just down the street from the theater?" she asked.

She passed the paper to my dad. He looked at it and whistled. "Anything for sale in that part of town is worth a small fortune."

I rolled one of my crusts up into a wheel before I asked, "How much would the theater sell for?"

Dad laughed. "A very big fortune! That's some of the most expensive land in the state."

"You children are lucky to have it," Mom said. "It's so beautifully landscaped."

My mother has to be the only person in the world who thinks the most important part of a theater is the plants that grow outside it.

I rubbed the small dark scab on my right thumb. It wasn't bleeding anymore but it still throbbed.

By the pricking of my thumbs,
Something wicked this way comes

"I've been thinking," I said quietly. "I may want to see what I can do besides acting at the Children's Theater."

My mother smiled one of her aren't-we-proud smiles at my dad. He smiled back as though he understood something she hadn't said yet.

"We thought you might want to try some new activities now that you're almost a teenager," she said.

Was it going to be this easy?

"I know a kid at the theater . . ." I started. My mother smiled again and nodded at me to continue. "She takes acting lessons in San Francisco, and I thought I might do that."

"Acting lessons? In The City?" By the tone of her voice, you'd think I'd said I wanted to poison the school drinking fountains or ride without a seat belt. "That's an hour's drive from here! How would you ever get there?"

My mother snapped her paper shut, got up, and began to clear the plates from the table. "That's just silly," she said in a tight voice.

My father turned his chair so he was looking straight into my eyes.

"Beth," he said in the persuasive, understanding tone he uses when he's practicing talking to a jury. "We've encouraged you to enjoy acting because it helps you build important skills—confidence, the ability to speak in front of people . . ."

"That means they think you're too shy," piped up R. J.

The kid's annoying even without a mouthful of tuna mush.

My father glanced at him in annoyance, but then he swiveled back to me again.

"If you ever become a lawyer," Dad continued earnestly, "all that practice speaking in front of people will be invaluable. But studying acting in The City is for someone who wants to become a professional actor."

He looked like he expected me to say something, but I didn't. So he spelled it out for me. "Acting's not that important to you, Scooter. It's just for fun."

I took a bite of sandwich and chewed it very slowly. I didn't taste anything. I didn't say anything, either.

"It's impossible," said my mother. "It's too far away."

You can always tell how upset Mom is by the amount of noise she makes. The dishes clinking showed she was at her unhappy-with-the-idea-but-not-taking-it-too-seriously level. When she's really upset, it gets much louder.

"And you don't need to go anywhere else to get the chance to act," she continued. She was smiling again and the dishes slipped quietly into the dishwasher. "You have the Children's Theater."

I couldn't finish my sandwich.

My bike clipped the edge of the large wooden sign that read LUCILLE BOW MEMORIAL PARK as I turned into the rack. The poor sign had been nicked so many times the right corner was worn away at the bottom. I always felt bad when I knocked into it. Lucille Bow was the person who gave all the money to build the Children's Theater zillions of years ago. It seemed ungrateful to run into her name.

Zandy was waiting for me in the lobby, sitting slumped against the far wall as though her bulging backpack had pulled her down to the ground. The handle of her tennis racket stuck out right over her head.

"You look like a unicorn," I said, sliding down the wall to join her. "Did you get a ticket for your dad?"

"He won't need it." Zandy's head was resting on her legs, so her voice sounded a bit mumbly.

"Your dad's going to usher?"

"My father can only manage to see me for one day," Zandy said, very clearly this time. "Sunday."

Our theater's dark on Sundays.

Zandy looked up, staring at the dust motes dancing in the beam of sunlight that shone through the window by the door.

"I asked him to come tonight or next week but he can't change his schedule," she said to the dust motes.

"Has he ever seen you perform?" I asked. I shouldn't have.

"No. Never."

She stood up, held her arm out as if she had a tennis racket in her hand, and took a couple of powerful swings

in the theater. I've read "13 Superstitions Every Theater Kid Should Know" so many times I think I've memorized it.

Mrs. Mac set the pencil down on her desk carefully. "Some of the superstitions are based on common sense. It was unlucky to whistle in a theater when retired sailors ran the rope gallery that controlled everything hanging over the stage. They communicated by whistles just like they did onboard ship. The wrong whistle and the scenery could come crashing down on your head." She looked at me directly. "But no sailors work backstage here."

"I know it's silly to worry." I glanced down at the floor, unable to meet her eyes. I felt like such a geek.

"What's silly is to worry without doing anything about it." She picked up the pencil and stuck it back in her hair. "If you believe in the jinx, you must believe in the cure. For a mention of the Scottish play, the speaker is supposed to go outside." She pointed to the door in her office that opened to the sidewalk. "Turn around three times and . . ." she paused for a long moment, as though she were unsure of what came next, then asked, "did you say the name?"

I shook my head. "I just quoted a line."

"So three turns should be enough. Widdershins," she added. "Counterclockwise."

I waited to hear the rest but all she said was, "Then knock on the door and beg to be let back in."

"That's all?" I asked.

She nodded, so I went outside, turned around three times, knocked on the door, and said, "Please, please, let me in." Zandy opened it for me and I stepped back into the office.

"That should lift the jinx," said Mrs. Mac, rescuing the pile of fabric samples from falling one more time. "Now, is there anything else that's troubling you?"

You could tell from her voice that she expected us to leave.

But we were there on a mission. Zandy looked at me hesitantly, then said, "We heard a rumor that the theater is closing."

Mrs. Mac didn't answer immediately, so I prompted her. "That's totally false, isn't it?" My voice rose on the last word.

"Not totally," Mrs. Mac said finally. She pulled another pencil out of her hair. Two taps on her desk, and she pointed it at the door to the hallway.

"Would you please close the door, Beth?" she said.

My stomach flopped. Mrs. Mac was supposed to deny the theater was closing. Ever.

I walked over, pushed the door slowly until I heard the latch click, then dragged my way back as if I was walking to my own execution.

Mrs. Mac slid the pencil back in her hair and waved her hand at two photographs hanging on the right wall.

"You know Lucille Bow built the Children's Theater almost fifty years ago?"

Of course. We both looked at the pictures. One showed Mrs. Bow standing with a bouquet at the curtain call for *Romeo and Juliet.* In the other she was seated among a sea of kids in the front row of the audience. In both shots she was wearing a fur stole and a little hat with a big veil. "She built it for the children of this city, but she didn't give the building to us. We rent it from her," Mrs. Mac went on.

"Didn't Mrs. Bow die a long time ago?" I asked at the same time as Zandy said, "Is the rent very expensive?"

Mrs. Mac smiled and answered us both. "She died about twenty-five years ago and her nephew inherited the lease. He wasn't very interested in us but we continued to pay our rent to him." She turned to Zandy. "It's only a peppercorn rent."

"Peppercorn?"

I'd just refilled our pepper grinder about a week ago. Either I hadn't heard correctly or I could pay the theater's rent for the next hundred years and my mom wouldn't even notice.

"A peppercorn rent means someone pays a very small amount. It could be one peppercorn," said Mrs. Mac. "In our case, it's a dollar a year."

"Then why does anybody think the theater is closing?" Zandy asked, grabbing the stack of samples that were threatening to topple off the desk once more.

Mrs. Mac took the pile from Zandy and placed it on the floor. "We have a fifty-year lease," she said as she straightened back up. "But it was signed over forty-nine years ago. It expires in six months, at the end of September."

"Can't we get a new one?" Zandy and I spoke almost simultaneously.

Mrs. Mac smiled. "The city is working on getting it renewed," she said. "It's taking longer because Edward Fredericks died just before he was going to sign the new lease. Then his widow inherited the theater." She looked down at her desk, picked up a yellow pencil, and put it down again before she leaned back in her chair. "Mrs. Fredericks may not have signed the lease *yet*, but the city expects that it will all be settled in a few weeks. I've talked to her," she added. "And you'll be happy to know she loves theater, asked lots of questions about ours, and is planning to visit us very soon."

"Could she sell the theater?" I demanded. "Tear it down and build really expensive houses?"

When Mrs. Mac laughed, I knew she wasn't laughing at me but at the impossibility of the idea. It made me feel better immediately. "Not a chance. Mrs. Fredericks may own the building, but the city owns the land. This site can only be used for a theater."

"What was that about some Scottish play?" Zandy demanded as soon as we left Mrs. Mac's office.

"It's a play by Shakespeare," I said. "I can't tell you the name because we're in a theater. But it's the most unlucky play ever. And I haven't lifted the jinx yet."

Any one who's memorized "13 Superstitions Every Theater Kid Should Know" would realize I'd left two things out. I don't know why Mrs. Mac didn't notice, but since she said it's silly to worry without doing anything about it, I pulled Zandy into the girls' bathroom, got a paper towel, wet it, and she and I headed for the lobby.

I went outside and turned three times. Widdershins, like Mrs. Mac said. This time, I spit and I cursed. Okay, really quietly so no one else could hear, but I cursed. Then I begged loudly to be let back in.

"What were you mumbling out there?" Zandy asked. She was Googling something on her phone.

"Nothing." I held up the paper towel. "I have to go clean my spit from the sidewalk. It's funny Mrs. Mac forgot that part."

"You know what's really funny?" said Zandy, staring down at the screen. "I just found a list of Shakepeare's plays. If the Scottish play is the one I think it is, then if you put Mrs. Mac's name and your name together, you've spelled it out."

CHAPTER FIVE

What think you of a duchess? have you limbs
To bear that load of title?

Shakespeare's *Henry VIII*

Lasagna has to be my favorite food. The smell of it baking grabbed me and drew me straight to the kitchen as soon as I walked through the door. It wasn't ready yet, so I was rummaging in the fridge looking for a snack—a very large snack—when my heartless mother ordered me away.

"You'll ruin your dinner."

"It's not for hours and I'm hungry." I lowered one shoulder, tilted my head at a pathetic angle, and moaned the last few words.

It didn't work.

"We're eating in thirty minutes so you can make your play. Scoot."

"Pleeease . . ."

My weak, pleading voice was clearly beginning to get to my mom. She loves to feed people. My odds of coming away from this with at least a small snack were growing, and we both knew it.

Then the phone rang. Mom grinned at me in triumph. She knew I couldn't bear to let it ring, and if I abandoned the refrigerator, she'd be able to resist any further pleas.

I stood there, hesitating, while R. J. walked by and picked up the receiver. His conversation was like a one-sided tennis match. "Hello. . . . Yes. . . . Okay." Then he handed it to me and said so loudly the person on the other side of the phone was bound to hear every word, "It's Mrs. Mac. What did you do wrong?"

All thoughts of food fled as I took the receiver.

"Tell your brother you didn't do anything wrong." There was a smile in Mrs. Mac's voice, then it became serious. "Lara Kindle has come down with the flu and won't be able to go on tonight. I'd like you to play the Duchess as well as the Cat. You're not in any of the same scenes and you'd have time to change costumes. Think you can do it?"

"Yes!"

"Then get here as soon as you can."

What an honor!

I was spending the night at Zandy's after the play, so I took one farewell sniff of the lasagna and got packed fast.

My parents are pretty good about theater emergencies, but my mom insisted on making me a sandwich before I left. My dad insisted that I wait until I got to the theater to eat it. Once when I was really young, I spilled a whole milkshake in the back of his brand new SUV. He hasn't let me eat in his car since.

It was pouring rain by the time Dad pulled up in front of the theater.

"Take my umbrella. You'll get soaked," he said.

I shook my head. "It's only ten feet to the breezeway."

I blew him a kiss, grabbed my backpack and the sandwich, said, "Thanks, Dad," and took off running before he could finish saying, "Don't slip on the wet pavement."

We're not allowed to take food into the theater. I wolfed half of the sandwich outside the door. My clothes had gotten so wet in the ten feet between the car and the breezeway, and the wind was so strong, I was shivering with cold. I kept hearing Mrs. Mac say, "Get here as soon as you can," so I tossed the rest of the sandwich in the trash can and ran into the lobby, still chewing.

Austin was lying in wait for me. He grabbed my arm before I got two steps through the door. "Mrs. Mac wants you to go to her office first," he said. "It's going to be a rough show. Another kid, one of the Mice, just called in sick."

"Cross your fingers that no one else gets it." I crossed my own as I said it.

"At least all my crew seem to be okay so far," he added as I hurried to Mrs. Mac's office. Austin believes firmly that the crew is the most important part of any play.

I couldn't touch the photo of Juliet with him in the lobby.

But I could come back.

I knocked on the door frame before I entered the office. Mrs. Mac peered over the piles on her desk, at least five pencils stuck in her hair this time.

"Thank goodness," she said as soon as she saw me, then leaned forward and studied me carefully. She sat back in her seat, pulled out a pencil, and began tapping off instructions. "Lara's much taller, so you can't wear her costume. Ask Mrs. Lester to pull a medieval gown for you. There must be at least thirty hanging in the rack room. Lara's was blue, so try to find one that color, but the most important thing is that it fits." The tapping stopped. "Can you think of any other problems you might have?"

Could I think of any other problems? Of course I could. It's bad luck to wear blue onstage. At least that's what "13 Superstitions Every Theater Kid Should Know" says. Sometimes I wonder if it's always right. I've seen a lot of blue costumes onstage, though I've never had to wear one. And then I remembered that Lara had worn a blue gown and she had come down with the flu after the first performance.

Maybe I could get away with wearing a dress in another color. After all, Mrs. Mac had only told me to *try* to find a blue gown.

That left only one other problem.

"How many lines does the Duchess have? After I get the costume and do my Cat makeup, I'm not going to have much time to learn them."

Mrs. Mac smiled at me and began rifling through the piles on her desk. "I knew I could count on you."

She pulled out a script and handed it to me.

"The Duchess only has three or four lines, but they're complex and very important to the comedy in the ball-room scene. Make an index card with the cues and your lines and carry it with you onstage."

"I can memorize it," I protested, but she interrupted me.

"Memorize what you can," she said. "You might be word perfect when you go on—you've always been a quick study—but these lines have to come in on exactly the right cue. It's not fair to the other actors to take a chance."

I couldn't argue with that.

"Hide the card in your skirt. If you need to look at it, I know you'll be able to think of some action to cover what you're doing." She paused and thought for a moment. Tap went the pencil. "No. All the Duchesses carry fans. Paste it in your fan and no one in the audience will know what you're using it for."

The phone rang just as she finished speaking.

"Break a leg," she said and gave me a little nod of dismissal as she reached to answer it.

I needed to hurry, but I headed straight back to the lobby. I glanced around casually just to make sure no one was there before I walked over to the back wall. I looked around once more then brushed my finger on the brass plaque underneath the old photograph.

"Someday," I whispered, and headed for the costume shop, smiling.

The costume shop looked absolutely normal for just before a performance. Prince Charming was heading out the door, wearing a gold crown and a cardinal-red Stanford sweatshirt, and buckling a jeweled sword over his jeans. Pam was getting the purple jewelry that she wore as the Stepsister out of the cabinet drawer, and Mrs. Lester was sitting at one of the sewing machines, mending a costume for a worried-looking Page Boy. When I told her I needed a medieval gown, she just pointed at the rack room.

Rack rooms were named after the long poles, or racks, that hang from their ceilings. You'd think they would be called costume rooms, because there are only a few poles—ours has six—that run the length of the room, while there must be thousands of costumes crammed on each one.

Somehow, in the mass of medieval gowns, I managed to find a lilac dress that looked about my size. It fit.

But when I showed it to Mrs. Lester, she started to frown. "What part are you playing?"

"One of the Duchesses. Lara's sick."

Mrs. Lester closed her eyes tightly together for a few seconds, then shook her head. "No, no. You'll be standing next to Nafeesa Russell. She's in lavender. That color is too similar." She opened her eyes again. "You need a light blue gown. Like Lara wore. Didn't Mrs. Mac tell you that?"

"She said the important thing was that it fit."

Mrs. Lester gave me a quizzical look. "And she didn't say anything about the color?"

Busted.

"Just to try to find a blue one."

"I suppose this shade does look almost blue," she said. "But can you see that it's more purple in this light?"

I bobbed my head, reluctantly. "Yes."

It looked like there was no way I was going to get out of wearing a blue costume. Mrs. Lester motioned me to follow her as she walked to the rack room.

"We'll find you the right color," she said, turning sideways to fit down the narrow aisle between the clown and animal costumes. The medieval gowns started at the back half of the left rack, right after a dozen spotted Dalmatian suits.

The first gown Mrs. Lester picked was huge. The second one, sky-blue brocade with a string of pearls looped across the bodice, fit perfectly.

Of course it did. According to "13 Superstitions Every Theater Kid Should Know," it's also bad luck to wear real jewelry onstage.

But surely the pearls were imitation.

"Mrs. Lester, are these real pearls?"

She crossed her arms and cocked her head. "Really, Beth? Thousands of dollars of pearls hanging in the rack room? Where do you think the term 'costume jewelry' comes from?"

I smiled at her. "Of course. They just look so pretty, you'd think they were real."

One down. One to go. "Mrs. Lester, have you ever heard that it's bad luck to wear a blue costume onstage?"

"What?" She sounded indignant. "I've never heard any such thing. And I've been a costumer for more than thirty years."

I felt a rush of hope. Our teachers are always telling us not to believe everything we read online. Maybe someone just made up the superstition about blue costumes being cursed. If Mrs. Lester hadn't heard of it, and Mrs. Mac had asked for a blue costume, it probably wasn't true.

"Can you imagine what my job would be like if I couldn't use blue?" Mrs. Lester reached into the costumes hanging on the other side of the aisle and pulled out the skirt of a deep blue gown with a white pinafore. "What would I put Alice in?" She dropped it and grabbed a dress of blue-and-white check. "Or Dorothy? Ridiculous!"

She marched out of the rack room and rummaged in a box on the wall marked HATS, MEDIEVAL. I followed behind her. She'd convinced me already, but she wasn't finished.

"I think most theater superstitions are silly, but that is the silliest one I've ever heard."

She tugged a small blue cap trimmed with pearls out of the box and popped it on my head. She backed up, put her hands on her hips, and ran her eyes over me from head to toe. Then she smiled.

"Perfect," she said and handed me a fan. "Find a pair of character shoes that fit and you're all set."

My heart sank.

I'd never worn character shoes before. They must have two-inch heels.

"Can't I just use the ballet slippers I wear with my Cat costume?"

I knew what Mrs. Lester was going to say before she said it. "All the Duchesses wear black character shoes."

"I'm not very good at walking in heels," I protested half-heartedly.

"Then you'd better start wearing them. You're going to need all the practice you can get."

I rushed up to the dressing room, wobbling all the way.

Zandy kept everyone from talking to me as I tried to do my makeup and learn my new part at the same time. There weren't that many lines, but the Duchess talked in tongue twisters. Whenever the King exploded in a one-word speech, I'd follow with a string of words starting with the same sound.

When he said, "Disappeared!" my line was, "A distinctly disturbing departure."

I had to practice saying all the lines out loud to make sure I didn't trip on any of them. The hardest was the one with the simplest words: "Find the fair female whose fragile foot it fits."

Naturally I had to say that one twice.

Fitting the lines on my fan was a tough job as well. There was only enough room for my lines and the cues that came right before them. Any line that repeated only got taped in once.

But I wasn't worried. I didn't have to know exactly where each cue came in the scene. I only needed to listen and react when the King spoke.

When the rest of the cast arrived, we ran through the scene onstage. The blocking was a piece of cake. The Duchesses always walked in a line, and I was at the end.

All I had to do was follow everyone until our exit, when we turned back the way we came in. Then I said, "Find the fair female whose fragile foot it fits," one last time and led us offstage.

No problem.

Because of all the changes, Mrs. Mac asked everyone to meet in the house for notes before we started. I like being in the house just before the play begins. There's such a feeling of expectation. The curtain is closed, waiting to be opened, and I always think the seats look eager for the audience to come in and claim them. Time for us to get our business done and back to our side of the curtain so the house manager can open the doors.

I managed to get my favorite seat in the second row, B-8 (B for Beth and eight—my lucky number). I was feeling pretty confident.

Mrs. Mac's notes took longer than usual because she had to announce that we'd be one Mouse short and that I was going to play a Duchess. She'd just finished working out the changes in the curtain call—as we went out onstage at the end of the performance, I was supposed to wear the Duchess's costume and carry my Cat headdress—when she dropped the bombshell.

"We'll be having a very special guest tonight," she said. "A relative of Lucille Bow, the woman who built the Children's Theater so many years ago, will be here. I know you'll enjoy knowing Marguerite Fredericks is in the audience. Mrs. Fredericks was married to Lucille Bow's nephew."

So, Mrs. Fredericks, who held the future of the theater in her hands, was watching this performance.

No problem. *Cinderella!* was a very good play.

Austin came up and told Mrs. Mac that a crew member was going home sick.

No problem. He'd find someone else to crew.

Zandy whispered that she'd just heard that our Cinderella, Emily Chang, had a temperature and wouldn't tell anyone how high it was.

No problem. Emily was famous for never missing a performance. She wasn't onstage every minute. She could throw up between scenes if she had the flu. I'd seen her do it once before when she was sick.

I was playing a part I'd only rehearsed once.

No problem. I had a copy of my lines pasted in my fan. I just followed all the other Duchesses onstage.

The play would be great.

No problem.

The performance started off with a bang. The Mice worked around the missing performer so well, no one in the audience could tell they were one short. My scene as the Cat fleeing the purple smoke got another great laugh.

I didn't fret about playing a part under-rehearsed. When the moment of reckoning arrived, I picked up my fan from the prop table and trotted gaily onstage with the other three Duchesses. I snapped my fan open, and my lines were right there in front of me. I just had to listen for the King to give my cues.

The first one came early.

"Disappeared!" said the King, and I immediately followed with, "A distinctly disturbing departure."

The line got a few laughs but it should have gotten a lot more. My character was there to provide comic relief.

I thought about how to play it a little bigger as I waited for my next cue. When it came, I threw my arms out and said, in a strong New York accent, "Talk, talk, tell us the tale of your travels."

The audience's laugh was longer and louder. I breathed a sigh of relief. I shouldn't have switched to an accent in the middle of the scene, but I figured no one would notice since I had only spoken four words without it.

I checked my fan. Only one more line but I had to repeat it twice.

A little Page had been moving slowly around the stage, holding out a tray of treats the King was serving in the ballroom. The Duchesses were last on his rounds. It wasn't until I reached over to take one that I realized the spongy yellow squares weren't foam rubber.

Most of the time stage food is fake. I guess the director thought it would make the ballroom scene more realistic if we actually ate.

"What is this?" I murmured through a gracious smile.

"Pound cake. It's great," he mouthed back, bowing.

I took a piece and popped it in my mouth. And my stomach took over. *More* was the message it was sending, loud and clear.

I snagged another before the Page passed down the line, serving the other Duchesses. When he was done, he came back and stood by me. That was convenient.

I helped myself to another piece.

And another.

I was starving, but eating didn't make me lose my concentration.

When the King said, "Forward," I flung my arms apart, turned on my New York accent, and said, "Find the fair female whose fragile foot it fits," with perfect timing. And with great aplomb spat three mostly chewed pieces of pound cake in a crumby shower all over the stage.

The Duchesses broke first. They tried to hide it behind their fans but everyone onstage knew they were laughing. And one by one all the other characters in the court scene began to break up. Voices were strained to cracking. Sudden gasps and at least one snort sounded as people let their breath out. The King spent a lot of time coughing into his hand.

I blushed. What would Mrs. Mac think of me? I heard her voice saying, "I know you'll be able to think of some action to cover what you're doing."

Since I'd just shown my character as a glutton, I'd continue to play her that way. I kept stuffing more of the pound cake in my mouth. The Page indignantly tried to move the tray out of my reach, so I grabbed his arm and kept eating.

This time I made sure to chew and swallow before another piece went in. When my last cue came, I faced the audience with a piece of cake in my hand. I was blowing out my cheeks so they looked like they were stuffed full of pound cake. The audience snickered in anticipation. I flung my arms apart, said, "Find the fair female whose fragile foot it fits," without spitting, and turned sharply to lead the Duchesses offstage.

I'm not used to turning sharply in high heels. I teetered and reached out for the Page's tray to balance myself.

He snatched it away.

I fell, but the audience loved it.

After I landed, I gave a great big grin and flung my arms out like it was deliberate—I was really checking for broken bones. It turned out I was fine.

But the beading on the front of my dress wasn't. One of the loops had broken and the pearls cascaded to the floor in a shower of pings.

Thirty years as a costumer! How could Mrs. Lester not know blue costumes were bad luck?

I stood up, regained my balance on the heels, clutched my bodice to try to stem the flow of pearls, said, "Find the fair female whose fragile foot it fits" once more, and led the Duchesses offstage.

On the way, I made a deep, deep curtsy to the King and managed to scoop up three of the pearls. Nafeesa realized what I was doing. She curtsied and picked up the last two. Part of acting is reacting to whatever happens onstage. All the other Duchesses added in a curtsy as they passed the King. It went as smoothly as if we'd rehearsed it.

Lesser actresses might despair at messing up a scene that badly, but not me. I had a plan. I'd persuade my father to move to Saudi Arabia—preferably tonight—and take me with him.

Chapter Six

And all the secrets of our camp I'll show,
Their force, their purposes; nay, I'll speak that
Which you will wonder at.

Shakespeare's *All's Well That Ends Well*

Mrs. Mac brought Mrs. Fredericks backstage after the play ended.

I didn't go into the lobby with the rest of the cast. I'd tried to mend the pearls on my dress with a piece of tape, but when I took the costume off, the pearls took off, too, all over the dressing room floor. The bad luck wasn't going to stop just because I was no longer onstage. I had to pick them up before someone slipped or fell.

Then that disastrous dress needed to go to the costume shop for repair. Even better would be to put it directly in the garbage can to keep some other poor actor from ever having to wear it again. But there was no way Mrs. Lester would let that happen. So I bundled it up, tucked it under my arm, and headed out the door, running right into Mrs. Mac.

She was the last person I wanted to see after I'd made such a fiasco as the Duchess. I couldn't meet her eyes until she bent over and whispered, "So sorry. I forgot to tell you to spit."

I looked up, grinning, and Mrs. Mac introduced the elegant woman in the pale suede suit who was with her.

"Mrs. Fredericks is interested in seeing our theater," Mrs. Mac said.

Other people nod; Mrs. Fredericks inclined her perfect blonde head.

"Austin is going to take Mrs. Fredericks on a tour of the backstage area," Mrs. Mac said and looked at her watch. "Unfortunately, I need to be in the lobby right now. Could you help him show her around?"

I was so happy Mrs. Mac trusted me after the mess I'd made onstage, I would have agreed to anything. And I wanted to make the woman who owned my theater happy any way I could.

"Would you like to see the dressing room while we wait for Austin?" I asked.

She inclined her head one more time. Somehow walking into the dressing room with Mrs. Fredericks made the old sock smell stronger than ever and the floor look even more cluttered.

She looked around quickly—there is not a lot to see in an empty dressing room—walked over to the mirror, and patted her pageboy. I don't know why, because no hair on her head would have dared leave its place.

Then she looked at me curiously and out of the icy blonde perfection came the strongest New York accent I've ever heard.

"Were you in the play?"

I stood there, clutching the bundled Duchess costume tightly, praying she wouldn't realize I was the one who had just mimicked an accent just like hers for comic relief.

"I played the Cat," I said, pointing at the cat head sitting on top of one of the racks.

"Oh, you're the funny one."

Mrs. Fredericks walked over and stroked the artificial fur on the headdress.

"Nice costume," she said. "Did you wear it for the curtain call? I don't remember seeing the Cat."

When I explained I was playing two parts, she looked startled.

"Isn't it hard for someone as young as you to do that?" she asked.

"We do it all the time if someone's sick," I answered.

Mrs. Fredericks was looking very impressed, until she asked me what other part I played.

"One of the Duchesses."

At that moment, another pearl slipped from the bundled-up dress I was holding in my arms and fell with a little ping to the floor.

Mrs. Fredericks looked down at the pearl and back up at me. "Oh, yes," she said flatly. "The one with the accent."

There didn't seem to be a lot to say after that. I shifted the dress to my other arm and Mrs. Fredericks fiddled with her bracelet.

This woman has to like us, I thought. *Say something nice.*

"What a pretty suit," I said.

"Thank you. A friend of mine designed it."

Her voice sounded a little warmer, so I tried again.

"That's an unusual bracelet."

She held out her arm so I could see it better. Ten big, tear-shaped stones glittered around a sparkling yellow circle.

"It's a daisy," she said. "My name, Marguerite, means 'daisy' in French."

"Pretty. So's your purse."

She gave me a half-smile, which told me to knock it off. "It matches the shoes. Now, why don't you tell me about the theater. Do you know how many people it seats?"

"Two hundred and forty-eight."

"Are you sure?"

I nodded. "If we're ushering, we have to count out two hundred and forty-eight programs before we open the doors to seat the audience."

Austin's knock on the dressing room door saved me from having to think of anything else to say. He walked us around the backstage areas, talking enthusiastically about every major piece of machinery and a lot of the minor ones, his hair sticking straight up as always. Mrs. Fredericks was really nice to him. She must have asked him at least one question per machine.

When Austin introduced her to Chuck Peterson, our technical supervisor, she paid them both the ultimate compliment: "This is as well-equipped as a professional theater." Austin and Chuck beamed.

We ended up in the middle of the stage, with Austin pointing at the row of thick ropes lining the wall of the right wing.

"The theater has a full rigging system," he said. "The ropes let us raise and lower flats when they're needed for each scene. If you look up, you'll see the backdrops for the sets used in *Cinderella!* hanging in the flies above you."

I leaned back and studied the wooden frames of the flats for the kitchen, the barnyard, and the ballroom hanging over my head. They might only be four inches thick—which is why they're called flats—but they're around twelve feet long and fifteen feet tall and the only things that kept them from sailing down on me were a few ropes and knots.

I almost let out a whistle but I caught myself. Even if we didn't have old sailors running our rigging system, there was no way I was whistling in a theater.

"Quite as well-equipped as a professional theater," Mrs. Fredericks said again.

You could tell she was very impressed.

By the pricking of my thumbs,
Something wicked this way comes

Why did that just pop into my head? I glanced up again. Just thinking about the flats crashing down must have triggered it.

"Would you like to go out on the catwalk?" Austin asked, then pointed up to the iron cage running along the ceiling in front of the curtain. "You have to crawl most of the way but you get the best view of the theater hanging up there over the orchestra pit."

I looked at Mrs. Fredericks's pale suede suit.

Mrs. Fredericks looked at her pale suede suit.

And one of the crew came out of the shop to show Austin the three-week-old cream cheese and jelly sandwich he had just found in his backpack. Mrs. Fredericks started to take a breath as though she wanted to speak, but it was very clear it wasn't a good idea to breathe right then, so she didn't say anything at all.

"Why don't I take you to the costume shop now?" I said.

It would be a relief to get rid of that bad-luck gown I was still lugging around—and an even bigger relief to get away from that sandwich.

The costume shop was crawling with Mice.

Mrs. Lester was sitting at one of the sewing machines, a pile of costumes to mend next to her and five little girls dressed as Mice in front of her. They were all speaking in high, agitated voices that sounded an awful lot like squeaking.

When Mrs. Fredericks and I walked in the door, a white Mouse turned around to look at us. "I lost my tooth," she said, holding it up proudly. The front of her costume was smeared with blood.

Mrs. Fredericks took a step back and almost got hit as the door opened again and Tina and Pam entered. They were both in jeans and sweatshirts. Pam was also wearing a rhinestone tiara, four or five long flashy necklaces, and a bunch of bracelets. Tina wore two tiaras and carried Zandy's Fairy Godmother wand.

The look of bewilderment on Mrs. Fredericks's face made me explain quickly, "Any part of the costume that might get lost, like jewelry or a wand, has to go back to the costume room after each performance."

By the time Tina and Pam began transferring their overload to the jewelry cabinet, Mrs. Lester had taken command. White Mouse was sent into the rack room to find another costume. Two of the other Mice were set to pick up straight pins—a constant job in the costume shop— while they waited for her. And the last two were sent back to the lobby to warn the waiting parents that some of the Mice would be a little late getting changed.

Molly was one of the Mice assigned to pin detail, but she asked to work on the mending instead. With a shake of her head, Mrs. Lester agreed, and I finally got to introduce her and Mrs. Fredericks.

"Welcome to the costume shop," Mrs. Lester said as they shook hands. "Do look around. If you want to see it in full operation, this is the perfect time to visit." She looked at my bundle. "And it looks like Beth's bringing something to add to the general confusion."

I couldn't say anything about blue costumes being unlucky with Mrs. Fredericks there. It would sound as though I was making excuses for my poor performance. I just handed the gown to Mrs. Lester and explained what had happened to the trim. I hardly needed to. Two more pearls slipped off when she spread out the costume.

"That's quite dangerous." Mrs. Lester picked up her scissors and snipped off the remaining loops while I searched for the two pearls that had escaped. I found them both, though I had to crawl under the sewing machine to retrieve the last one. "We'll have to find something besides pearls to trim this with," she added, putting the gown on the top of her mending pile.

Mrs. Fredericks drifted around the room, opening closet doors, poking in drawers and cabinets. You would think she was getting ready to buy the place.

Mrs. Lester's attention was back on the White Mouse, who had just come out of the rack room wearing a brown costume and carrying the bloody one.

"Perfect fit," Mrs. Lester said. She took the white costume, stuck it in the dry cleaning basket, and walked over to a box marked Tights, Brown. She pulled out a pair and handed them to the Mouse.

"Hang these in the dressing room with your new costume so you'll have them for the next show. But come down here first to see if the white one is back from the cleaners. If it isn't, wear the brown."

The Mouse who'd lost her tooth scampered off with the Mouse who'd been picking up pins, while Mrs. Lester walked over to her tiny office and wrote something down on a pad. "I've got to drop off the dry cleaning tonight," she was muttering, mostly to herself. "Blood sets if it's allowed to sit too long."

Mrs. Fredericks took the opportunity to walk over and look around Mrs. Lester's office. She was glancing at the plaques and pictures hanging on the wall when she suddenly leaned over to examine one more closely.

"Marilyn J. Lester?" She looked at Mrs. Lester, who nodded. "You have an MFA in Costume Design from New York University." Mrs. Fredericks's voice sounded like she was accusing Mrs. Lester of a crime, but I think some of that was her accent. "I thought you were a teacher."

Mrs. Lester laughed and shook her head. "Whatever gave you that idea? I'm just the wardrobe mistress."

"You work so well with children, I just assumed . . ." Mrs. Fredericks sounded puzzled. "You trained at NYU. Did you ever work with an adult company?"

"I costumed a show or two off-Broadway before I moved to California. Then I was at the San Francisco Opera for a few years."

Mrs. Fredericks broke in, her voice excited. "I may have seen one of the shows you did. My husband and I have . . ." She stopped and corrected herself. "I have season tickets for the Public Theater and Circle in the Square, but my husband and I saw a lot of off-Broadway shows when he was alive."

I perked up when I heard that. Those were some really big names in theater. Mrs. Fredericks must be a serious fan. It looked like the Oakfield Children's Theater was safe.

I couldn't wait to tell Zandy.

I suddenly remembered she and her mother were waiting for me in the lobby. I bit my lip, wondering what to do. Mrs. Fredericks didn't look ready to leave anytime soon, and Mrs. Lester seemed to be settling in for a long chat. They were talking about the operas Mrs. Lester had worked on.

"Why did you leave the Opera?" Mrs. Fredericks asked suddenly.

"I lived in Oakfield and hated the commute to The City. When this job opened up, and I found out I could design every show, I jumped at it."

"Did you find it hard to . . . to . . ." Mrs. Fredericks was using her right hand to help her search for the right word. She patted the air beside her hip as if she was indicating the height of a three-year-old. ". . . downsize?"

Mrs. Lester smiled. "To making smaller costumes?"

"I meant working with children instead of a professional company." Mrs. Fredericks seemed to have forgotten Molly and I were in the room. I had a feeling she wasn't used to noticing kids much.

"I like working with kids. There's a joy and enthusiasm—"

Mrs. Fredericks interrupted her again. "But it's only play. They're not training to become professionals. It's just for fun."

She remembered suddenly that I was there and glanced at me, a little embarrassed. "Don't get me wrong. I think it's great you kids are learning about theater. But no one here is going to be an actor when she grows up."

I felt myself blushing.

"They're certainly not encouraged to become professional actors. No one would encourage a child—or an adult—to go into such a hard field." Mrs. Lester seemed to be enjoying the discussion, too. "But now and then someone comes along who can't help it." *Did she glance over at me?* "If they want it enough, they'll do it anyway."

"Don't you find they have very little sense of responsibility at this age? Look at the stack of costumes that need repair." Mrs. Fredericks nodded at Molly, who was still stitching away.

Mrs. Lester followed her glance. "Your parents are waiting for you. It's time to go."

"I just finished," Molly said, laying her mending down on the cutting table.

Mrs. Lester shooed me out with her. "Go meet your ride. I promise I'll show Mrs. Fredericks every inch of the costume shop unless . . ." She turned to Mrs. Fredericks. "Is someone waiting for you?"

Mrs. Fredericks shook her head. "I find I'm traveling by myself these days."

🎭

Zandy was under a tree in front of the theater sitting on a bench, tucked in her mother's arm, looking happy. I apologized for keeping them waiting but her mother just smiled at me.

"It's such a beautiful night now that the rain has stopped," she said. "You can smell the orange blossoms so strongly. Want to join us?" She moved over to make room.

Sitting in the moonlight breathing in the achingly sweet scent of orange blossoms made me feel as if there were no problem in the world worth worrying about. Long ago, before the theater was built, before the land became a park, this was the site of an old Spanish hacienda. There's a historical plaque on the theater that tells about the early building. The family who lived there had planted oranges, and one old gnarled tree survived. It grew in front of the theater, its waxy white flowers glowing in the dark.

The sound of heels tapping along the old brick walkway broke the quiet. Mrs. Fredericks passed us heading to the parking lot.

The lights inside the theater went out, but we sat for a few more minutes, just long enough to hear the sound of heels tapping on the brick again. The sound grew louder, more urgent, until Mrs. Fredericks rushed past us and began beating on the theater door.

The lights came back on and we could hear voices, though we were too far away to distinguish anything being said. Then the door opened and Mrs. Fredericks disappeared inside.

Zandy's mother stood up suddenly and hugged herself, rubbing her arms briskly. "Time to go before we all freeze," she said and bobbed her head toward the theater. "Unless I miss my guess, that poor woman just lost her car keys."

I knew Mrs. Fredericks wasn't poor, but I also knew this was a golden opportunity to get her to like us.

"Let's look for her keys on the way to the car, just in case she dropped them."

Zandy's mom smiled at me and then at her daughter. "What a nice friend you have," she said.

Zandy winked at me. She knew what I was thinking.

CHAPTER SEVEN

We two alone will sing like birds i' th' cage.

Shakespeare's *King Lear*

I'd been curled up on the guest bed in Zandy's room for half an hour, but she was still trying on clothes, still looking for the perfect thing to wear to lunch with her father. Her bed was piled so high with her discards, I couldn't even see the pink and white striped bedspread that lay under it all—which was a shame, because her mother had hired a decorator to redo Zan's bedroom as a thirteenth birthday present, and under all the clutter it looked like something you'd see in a magazine.

I still remember when Zandy told me what her mom was giving her. I was so impressed; my parents' idea of redecorating my room is to tell me to make my bed.

Zandy held up a red jacket with a black ribbon trim. "Should we wear heels?" she asked.

"Did you see me wearing heels tonight? See this bruise?" I held up my arm. "Besides, we don't own any."

"I have a pair."

"Really?" This was news to me.

"I had to wear them when I was singing with that choir last Christmas. You could buy some."

"By lunchtime tomorrow? I have to go to church in the morning."

Zandy rummaged around in her closet again.

"How about pants?" she asked.

"How about wearing your Fairy Godmother eyelashes?" I said with a big yawn.

Zandy threw a shoe toward me but missed on purpose.

"Just because you don't have any problems," she said, "doesn't mean the rest of us can't use a little help."

"What do you mean?" I sat up indignantly. I did not appreciate hearing this from my best friend. "What about the theater closing?"

"You just told me Mrs. Fredericks loves theater and really liked ours when she toured it. Of course she's not going to close it."

"Mrs. Mac said she hasn't signed the lease yet."

"Beth, what else can the woman do with a two-hundred-forty-eight-seat theater in the middle of a public park?"

What else could she do with it?

I lay back into the pillows slowly, stress ebbing away, but then I bolted upright again.

"Don't forget how badly I messed up as the Duchess," I said.

"You won't have to play the Duchess again. There isn't another performance till Thursday and Lara's bound to be over the flu by then."

I sank back down again. The pillows felt so cool and soft. Zandy was right. What else could she do with a working theater in the middle of a public park?

Zandy pulled a blue dress the color of sapphire from the middle of the heap on her bed and held it in front of her for the third time.

"Does this make me look older?" she asked.

"Why would you want to look older?" I snuggled down further under the quilt. I'd gotten to bed so late the night before. And there was no reason to stay awake worrying. Zandy wasn't going to wear that pretty blue dress onstage.

"I want my father to see I'm not a kid anymore," she said in a small tight voice.

I opened my eyes and concentrated on the pattern of pink and blue roses on the wallpaper along the top of the wall. "I think my father likes to think of me as a little girl," I said hesitantly.

"Not mine." Zandy shook her head decisively. "He doesn't like being around kids."

Maybe there's no such thing as a life without problems. Some of them keep popping up no matter how hard you try to pretend they're not really there.

"It's not that easy to make fathers happy," I said slowly. "My dad doesn't like theater very much. Or at least he doesn't like me being around theater."

"He comes to all your shows."

"He liked it when I was little, but it's been different since I entered middle school. And I get lawyer stuff shoved down my throat all the time. Maybe if I played Portia . . ."

"Who?" Zandy pushed the pile of clothes to one side so she could sit on her bed.

I looked over to see if she was kidding, but she really didn't know who Portia was.

"You've got to read more Shakespeare," I said.

Zandy made a face at me.

"There's a famous female lawyer called Portia in *The Merchant of Venice*. My dad mentions her a lot when he talks to me, but he's not thinking of me playing the part."

"Does your mom mind you acting?"

"She was thrilled when I finally got in a show. They both were. And then proud when I started getting cast most of the times I tried out. But lately it's changed. It seems the better I get, the unhappier they get." I said the last sentence slowly. I hadn't realized that before I heard myself say it.

"Did you tell them you wanted to be an actor?"

"This morning I asked if I could take acting lessons in San Francisco." I turned my face into the pillow and blew a pink-checked ruffle out of my mouth.

"Great! What did they say?"

"They said San Francisco was too far. Only people who are serious about acting go all that way to study." Funny, my voice sounded as small and tight as Zandy's did when she was talking about her father. "They said it's not for someone who's just doing it for fun."

There was a long silence.

"You need to tell your parents you're serious."

"It's hard." I bit my lip. "It's going to make them unhappy."

And what makes me think I'm good enough?

"You're going to have to tell them sometime," said Zandy. "It's the only thing you've ever wanted to do."

"I wanted to drive a garbage truck when I was three."

This time it was a pillow that flew across the room.

"Zan." I was serious again. "Your dad . . . it'll get better. You're growing up."

Zandy stood up and grabbed an armload of clothes off her bed. She dumped it on her chair, stood back, and stared at the towering pile.

"The blue dress and heels," she said.

My parents picked me up to go to church at 9:30 in the morning. By the time we got back home, Zandy had left five messages on the answering machine, all about what she was wearing.

She and her dad rang our doorbell at one o'clock on the dot. Zandy'd ended up wearing the sapphire blue dress with stockings and heels after all. She looked great. She hardly even wobbled.

Her dad was in jeans and a knit shirt. He kept smiling really hard, but when he saw me in the dress I wore to my cousin's wedding, a little frown appeared between his eyebrows.

"I remembered how much Zandy loved to go to Pizza Pals and watch the puppets performing," he said. "But if you two would rather go somewhere else . . ."

"It's fine, Dad," said Zandy.

I smiled really hard, too, so he'd know it was okay with me. If we were watching the puppet show, we wouldn't have to talk.

But when we reached the restaurant and sat down at the benches around our table, the show hadn't started yet. Zandy's father tried to make conversation. He asked the usual questions grown-ups ask when they have no idea what to say to kids.

"What grade are you in, Beth?"

"Seventh," I said, looking down at the menu. "Same as Zandy."

"What's your favorite subject? Besides recess." He forced a laugh.

I'd read about a hollow laugh, but I'd never heard one before now.

"English."

"Same as Zandy," he said.

I glanced over at her. She was smiling the same big smile as her dad and twirling her hair. Zandy likes math and music and science. English is dead last on her list of favorite subjects.

Zandy's dad started in again after the pizza was delivered. "What do you want to be when you grow up, Beth?"

I looked at my pizza slice. The mushrooms and olives were different shapes, different sizes. The mushrooms were half circles with a stem, the olives were smaller, perfectly round.

"I don't know," I said.

I couldn't tell my own father the answer to that question. There was no way I was going to tell someone else's.

The afternoon could have been worse. No one died. The theater didn't burn down. Aliens didn't take over the Earth. But it was painful.

We were watching the Pizza Pal puppets perform for the second time when the miracle happened. A little girl, about four, hugging a very tattered stuffed mouse, came up to our table. All three of us watched her out of the corner of our eyes as she stared at Zandy, then ran back to her mother and tugged at her hand, talking excitedly. The mother looked over at us—by then we were all staring at her daughter—smiled apologetically, and let her little girl pull her over to our table.

"Did you play the Fairy Godmother in *Cinderella!* last week?" the mother asked Zandy.

Zandy nodded. "Yes."

"Could you give my daughter your autograph? I was afraid to disturb you but Hannah, that's my little girl, just insisted. She loved your performance so much."

Zandy smiled at them both, a real smile this time. "Well, sure," she said. "But . . ." She held out her empty hands.

The mother handed Zandy a napkin and a pen and turned to speak to Zandy's father. "You must be so proud of your daughter. She has such a beautiful voice. And her stage presence is extraordinary. We were so excited when we realized she was sitting here."

Zandy's father looked a little surprised. "I certainly am proud of her," he said.

I'm sure Zandy heard him all right but instead she concentrated on Hannah. "Did you like *Cinderella!?*" Zandy asked as she signed her name.

Hannah bobbed her head, gripping the stuffed mouse by its long tail.

"Do you remember the big Cat?"

Hannah bobbed again and stuck her thumb in her mouth.

"Would you like to have the Cat sign your napkin, too?"

Hannah shook her head vigorously.

Her mother smiled at me apologetically. "The Cat was a little scary if your favorite toy is a stuffed mouse."

Hannah never said anything. But as she walked back to her table, she was showing her mouse the napkin with Zandy's signature.

"Tell me about your singing," said Zandy's father, sounding really interested for the first time that day.

And Zandy—Zandy the perfectly mannered, Zandy the self-assured, who talks to adults with ease and grace—looked down at her plate as if she were . . . me.

So I told him.

I told him how the applause grew when she came out for her curtain call in *Cinderella!*. I told him how she got the title role in *Oliver!* even though she was a girl, and I told him how she kept getting parts that usually went to older kids because of her great voice.

Her dad listened like I was telling the most interesting story he'd ever heard.

Then he turned to Zandy and said, "Did your mother ever tell you how we met?"

She shook her head.

"We were both singing in our college choir. She had such a beautiful voice."

"Do you still sing?" she asked, and suddenly they were talking about music just like they'd been doing so for years.

I watched the puppet pals for the third time, nodding occasionally while Zandy and her dad chatted on. Half of what they were saying went over my head. Then they started singing little snatches of songs to each other above the din. The show ended just as Zandy's dad was singing, "Oh, what a beautiful morning . . ." In the sudden quiet, his voice boomed out to the whole restaurant, and Zandy collapsed in giggles.

Her dad ran his hand through his hair, embarrassed, but he grinned at his daughter while he was doing it. "I'd like to see you perform sometime."

Zandy shrugged, the laughing stopped.

He noticed and thought for a minute. "Some people on the project owe me a few favors. Why don't you call me, collect, as soon as you know you're going to be in another show. I'll do my best to swing a trip back to see you."

When they dropped me off, Zandy walked me to my door, her eyes shining with happiness. "Thanks," she said, then grabbed my arm and added fiercely, "Beth, we've got to save our theater."

CHAPTER EIGHT

Search for a jewel that too casually
Hath left mine arm

Shakespeare's *Cymbeline*

My mom was out in the garden, planting a flat of sweet peas and singing along to rock music blaring from her portable radio. I stopped and listened for a moment to the musical abilities of the woman who gave birth to me.

No wonder I didn't sing as well as Zandy.

When Mom saw me, she stood, arching her back and groaning a little. "When did Zandy start wearing heels?" she asked.

"Today."

She held out her muddy hands. "Want a hug?"

I backed away in mock terror. "Gardeners don't get hugs."

She stretched, groaning again. "At least tell me about your luncheon. Did you go somewhere snazzy?"

"Pizza Pals."

"Oh de . . . lightful." My mom's got pretty good manners, too. "I'm sure you and Zandy had a good time together. You always do."

I could tell she was looking for a way to change the subject and her face lit up when she thought of one. "Mrs. Mac wanted you to call her as soon as you got back."

"On a Sunday?"

The lines from the Scottish play sprang into my head. The theater was always dark on Sunday and Monday.

"It sounds like a pretty minor emergency. Someone lost a bracelet at the theater last night."

"A bracelet? Not car keys?"

My mom looked at me, puzzled. "I thought Mrs. Mac said a bracelet. But call her before you go over in case they found it already."

They hadn't.

Austin had been searching for an hour before I got to the theater. He filled me in on the details.

"We're looking for a bracelet with white and yellow diamonds set in the shape of a daisy." He ran his fingers through his hair, which sprang back up as soon as he took his hand away. "I didn't know diamonds came in yellow."

"Those were real!" I stared down at my wrist, remembering the size of the bracelet Mrs. Fredericks had showed me. "It must have cost a mint."

"Mrs. Fredericks is really bummed. She noticed it was gone as soon as she got to the parking lot last night. She went back to the theater and Mrs. Mac and Chuck Peterson helped her look for hours. They thought you and I might be able to trace exactly where we'd taken her."

So Austin and I went over every inch of the theater, retracing our steps from the previous night. I started in the girls' dressing room, crawling on my hands and knees to check under the makeup table, then under each rack of costumes. Nothing. After I was done, Austin checked the room again. We double-checked each other as we followed the route we had taken, step-by-step. The costume shop took the longest time because we had to search through all the boxes and baskets lying open. Every time we turned around we found another one, on a shelf or a table or pushed under a sewing machine. I looked through thirteen boxes and eight baskets before we were done, all filled with shoes or scraps of fabric, reels of every colored thread. We searched through each one in case the bracelet had fallen in and slipped to the bottom. Austin saw something glittering halfway down the last box of ballet shoes and dove for it. He stood up, holding a silver gum wrapper.

"Parking lot next?"

"We've looked everywhere else." Then a thought came to me. "The catwalk! Did she decide to . . ."

Austin just raised his eyebrows and stared at me with a pained expression.

"Parking lot."

We stopped by Mrs. Mac's office to tell her we were going outside. She was on the phone, so we pointed to each other and then to the lobby door. Not the hardest thing I'd ever had to pantomime. She nodded at us and mouthed, *Thank you.*

Austin and I walked between the theater and the parking lot twice but again we found nothing. Not even a gum wrapper.

We went back through the lobby and sat down in the dark auditorium, in the last row on the right. The only light shone from the single bulb of the ghost light. The ghost light is put onstage before all the other lights are turned off. It stays on to give the crew enough light to leave the theater and see their way back the next day.

Austin slumped down in his seat, dejected. "Think someone stole it?"

"No," I said, firmly. "I can't imagine Mrs. Lester or Mrs. Mac or Chuck Peterson taking it. And except for them, only kids were backstage. And what would a kid do with a big diamond bracelet?"

"If Mrs. Fredericks dropped it outside the theater, anyone could have stolen it. Then we'll never find it."

There was nothing to say to that.

We sat in silence, wondering how Mrs. Fredericks would react if she didn't find her bracelet.

Suddenly the work lights went on and Mrs. Fredericks walked out onto the stage with Mrs. Mac close behind her. Austin and I sat noiselessly in the shadows. It was like being in the audience during a play, only they didn't know we were watching.

"Beth and Austin searched this area before they went home," said Mrs. Mac.

Mrs. Fredericks pursed her lips but didn't say anything.

Austin and I looked at each other, puzzled. Then it dawned on me. I leaned over and whispered, "Mrs. Mac thought we were leaving! She doesn't know we're still here."

Great pantomime job we'd done. I hung my head and stared at my knees. If I couldn't communicate one simple message through my body language, why did I think I could ever become an actor?

Mrs. Mac and Mrs. Fredericks scoured the stage without saying another word, going over all the places Austin and I had looked. The silence went on so long it almost had a sound of its own.

Finally Mrs. Fredericks straightened up and rubbed the small of her back. "We're beating a dead horse. It's not here."

There was the tiniest of rustles as Austin and I slid down even further in our seats.

"I'm going back to New York on Wednesday. You have my phone number at the hotel if you find my bracelet before then."

Mrs. Fredericks walked to the front of the stage and looked out over the dark auditorium, her hands in the pockets of the most beautifully fitting slacks I'd ever seen. "If one of the kids has it and comes to you, don't scare them. All I want is my bracelet back. My lawyer will be contacting you about posting a reward."

She turned and started to walk offstage but Mrs. Mac stepped in front of her. "And your decision is final?"

Mrs. Fredericks nodded decisively. "I have an appointment with my lawyer first thing Monday morning. As I told you, I'll be instructing him to begin eviction proceedings at once."

I heard someone, me or Austin or both of us, draw in a breath with a tiny gasp.

Mrs. Mac's shoulders slumped. She looked away from Mrs. Fredericks for a moment, then straightened her back and said briskly, "If the bracelet is an issue here, I'm sure we could arrange to replace it . . ."

Mrs. Fredericks interrupted her angrily, waving her hand in the air. "It's irreplaceable. That bracelet was the last present my husband gave me before he died. He can never give me another one. He's gone and it's gone and . . ."

Mrs. Fredericks stopped and turned to look out at the auditorium again, breathing deeply as though she was fighting to get control of her voice. "And I miss him so much," she whispered to the dark auditorium, just loud enough that Austin and I could hear her.

By now we were both sitting so low in the seats, no one could have seen us, but we scrunched down even more, just in case.

Mrs. Fredericks turned back to face Mrs. Mac. "All I can do is try to keep his name alive," she said. "Theater meant a great deal to us both. As soon as I found out I inherited this theater, I decided to turn it into a memorial to him."

"The Oakfield Children's Theater could easily become the Edward Fredericks Children's Theater." Mrs. Mac reached out to touch Mrs. Fredericks arm in a gesture of sympathy, but Mrs. Fredericks pulled away from her.

"A children's theater isn't good enough. Not for him." Her voice cracked. "He has no connection to this type of theater. He loved the real thing—challenging memorable plays with great actors. That's why I'm going to find an adult company, a professional one with an outstanding reputation, and offer this theater to them."

They exited the stage, their voices fading as they left the wings.

Austin and I sat in silence for a minute or two, and as we did, the lines from the Scottish play left me. I wouldn't think of them again for months. But the line that replaced them was even worse.

A children's theater isn't good enough.

I'd heard the conviction in Mrs. Fredericks's voice as she said it. She was going to close our theater.

The work lights went off and the dim beacon of the ghost light shone just enough for us to find our way out.

We didn't speak till we got to the bike racks.

"If we don't tell anyone," I said, just before we started for home, "maybe it won't come true."

What do you do when your world starts to fall apart?

Call your best friend.

But Zandy was still out with her father. Her mom said she'd have her call me back, unless she got home after nine.

"Please ask her to call even if it's late," I begged. "I have a question about our English homework that's urgent."

Parents always buy that one.

When the phone finally rang, I must have jumped three feet. It was just after nine, so I knew I could only talk for a minute.

"Major disaster," I said. "I really, really wish I could see you tonight but . . ."

There was a short pause, while Zandy figured out what I really, really wanted to tell her.

"Me, too," she said, then added, "the English homework is to finish chapter eight for tomorrow's discussion. The quiz is on Tuesday."

Her mother had to be standing right next to her.

I went to bed early and lay awake, every muscle tense, listening to the late night sounds in the house: my parents getting ready for bed, their soft snores, and then their loud ones. By the second loud snore, I was out the window and on my way to Zandy's.

If I kept this up, I'd forget how to use the front door.

🎭

"We can't let her take our theater away," Zandy sounded so forceful I could almost believe we had a chance to save it.

"Shh," I whispered. "Your mom will hear us."

I leaned back on the wall next to her bed, exhausted. It had been a long day. Church, lunch with Zandy's dad, searching the theater, and now another late night bike ride.

I was okay until I told Zandy what Austin and I had seen . . . and heard. Putting it into words convinced me my theater was gone. I closed my eyes and let my head drop forward. I didn't have any energy left to fight. We had lost our theater.

But Zandy sounded ready to lead a battle.

"Mrs. Fredericks may own the theater," she said, much more quietly but just as intensely, "but the city owns the land. It's going to look really bad to evict kids from a theater in a city park and hand it over to some grown-ups."

I was too tired to nod, and she couldn't see me in the dark anyway.

"Especially when we've used it for fifty years." I could hear Zandy twirling her hair around her finger so fast I half expected to see sparks flashing. "Maybe if we call the news-papers, or the TV news station, they could take pictures of the eviction. If people see all our costumes and stuff just dumped on the sidewalk, I bet they'd be mad. And our parents and all the theater kids from the last fifty years, everyone who's ever worked in the theater, would protest it. There must be thousands of us."

I sat up and whispered urgently, "We can't tell any-one! Not until we hear this officially from Mrs. Mac or somebody. Now it's just information we learned by eavesdropping."

"But the eviction starts tomorrow!" Zandy protested.

We both sat quietly for a few minutes, Zandy twirling, me biting my lip.

What will happen to the picture of Romeo and Juliet? I wondered.

"Think she decided to take away the theater because she was mad about the bracelet?" Zandy finally whispered.

"It sure didn't help. But I don't think she likes kids that much. She'd made up her mind long before then. She wants a professional company in our theater. Adult actors."

And Austin and I had shown her , again and again, that this would be possible as we kept pointing out just how good our theater was. Just as good as a professional one.

Zandy and I sat in silence listening to each other's breathing. I was thinking about everything I'd lose when the theater closed. I know Zandy was, too. She and her father had just begun to know each other—they might never find another way to connect. He'd talked about coming to one of her shows, but if the theater closed, she wouldn't be in another play until after we were in high school. Will he still want to see her perform more than a year from now? Or will he have lost interest by then?

I heard Mrs. Fredericks's voice in my head: "A children's theater isn't good enough. Not for him." Even in my memory, her words cracked with emotion. We didn't have a chance.

But Zandy hadn't heard the finality in Mrs. Fredericks's voice.

"She probably doesn't even know who to give the theater to," she persisted. "I bet all the famous acting companies she knows are in New York and have their own theaters already or won't want to move all the way across the country to a small town in California. She'd change her mind if we found her bracelet."

I opened my eyes and sat up straight. Was there hope?

"But how can we find it?" I asked.

Since neither of us had any ideas, the conversation stalled again, till Zandy asked the same question Austin had. "Could someone have stolen it? Found it and took it and sold it?"

"But everyone who was backstage wants the theater to stay open. And who would know where to sell stolen jewelry?"

"Everybody knows you take stolen goods to a fence. Like Fagin in *Oliver!*."

"Knowing a fence in a play isn't going to help."

"It was based on a famous book by Charles Dickens." Zandy sounded a little indignant.

"Which was written more than one hundred years ago," I reminded her. "Do you really think anyone at the theater knows a fence? Or would recognize real diamonds, especially ones that big? I didn't when Mrs. Fredericks showed them to me."

Zandy made a small sound of agreement. "Maybe we could post a picture of it on the call board? One of the little kids might have picked it up, didn't know it was valuable, and kept it just because it was pretty."

"We better hope that didn't happen, because they'd probably lose it."

I had a horrible vision of one of the little Mice finding the bracelet on the floor, putting it in her backpack, and leaving the backpack and bracelet in her school cubby till the end of the year, when it would be thrown out and disappear forever. I shook my head to make the scene go away.

"That's why we have to return our costume jewelry to the shop every night," said Zandy. "They're afraid we'll lose it."

It's true—your jaw really does drop open when you're totally surprised.

I closed my mouth and grinned in the darkness. "Would you repeat that?"

"That's why we have to return our jewelry . . . to the shop . . . every night." Zandy had a matching grin. I could hear it in her voice.

"If you saw a big, shiny bracelet lying around backstage after the play, what would you do?"

"Pick it up, take it to the costume shop, and plunk it right in the drawer of the jewelry cabinet."

Suddenly I wasn't tired at all. We both knew exactly where that bracelet was.

Now we had a new problem. How did we tell Mrs. Mac?

This one we could solve.

"Do you know Mrs. Mac's home phone number?" I asked.

"No. Can't we call her at the theater?"

"She won't be there. Tomorrow's Monday. The theater's dark."

"Mrs. Mac needs to get that bracelet back to Mrs. Fredericks in time to stop the eviction," I reminded her.

"We'll have to email her. Now."

"Do you know her home email?"

"No. Can't we email her at the theater?"

"Even if she's there tomorrow, the eviction people may not let her in to use her computer. Or her phone."

"Do you know where she lives?"

"No."

"What else can we do?" The excitement was gone from Zandy's voice.

"If you were going to break into the theater," I asked slowly, "who would you get to help you?"

CHAPTER NINE

Then how or which way should they first break in?
Question, my lords, no further of the case,
How or which way: 'tis sure they found some place
But weakly guarded, where the breach was made.

Shakespeare's *Henry VI, Part 1*

Who would I ask to help me break into the theater?" Zandy gave a small groan of pure misery. She hates doing anything her mother wouldn't like. But the answer to my question was so obvious, she replied to the one I hadn't asked yet. "It's too late to call Austin now."

So we texted him.

We knew Austin. Ultimate techie. He'd never turn off his cell phone. Even if he was asleep, he'd get the message.

He must have been awake because his answer came back immediately: I CAN GET US IN. MEET BACK PORCH.

Zandy and I gave ourselves a high five. A quiet high five. It looked like all our problems were solved.

We'd been pretty sure Austin would help. The theater meant as much to him as it did to us, only in a different way. Where else could he use power tools, run electrical wiring, or program a lighting board? He'd loved showing off the backstage to Mrs. Fredericks. Of course he was going to help us.

Five minutes later, we were wheeling our bikes down the driveway. I suppose we should have felt as carefree and happy as all those kids in books who sneak out at night and have wonderful adventures—from Tom Sawyer to the Berenstain Bears. But Zandy had never snuck out at night before and she jumped at every sound. It didn't help that it began to rain so hard we could barely keep our bikes on the road. We were dripping wet by the time we arrived at the small porch on the back of the theater. We stashed our bikes in the bushes and huddled together under the little roof covering the door.

"Where's Austin?" Zandy whispered anxiously.

We saw him almost as soon as she spoke. He was as soaked as we were. We waited for him to drop his bike beside ours, but he rode it up onto the porch and leaned it against the wall. He grinned at us, pulled a can out of his jacket, and shook it vigorously.

"You're going to have to hold my bike so I can climb up," he said.

"What are you doing?" demanded Zandy. "Where's the key?"

"What key?" Austin stopped shaking the can, a puzzled look on his face.

She pointed at the door. "You said you could get us in."

"Yeah," he said slowly. "But I don't have a key to the door."

"Then how are we going to get inside?" She was starting to sound mad.

"There's a padlock on the flat house. I've had to open it so many times I've got the combination memorized. We're going in through there."

"Then why are you messing around over here?"

"Because I've got to disable the alarm before we go inside," he said and pointed the can at a round metal square mounted high on the wall. "I'm going to squirt shaving cream in that box. The foam should muffle the noise when the alarm starts ringing." He grinned and started shaking the can again. "I read about this on a website. I've always wanted to try it."

I was afraid Austin was enjoying himself too much.

It looked like Zandy thought so, too. She crossed her arms and narrowed her eyes. "Just why are you worrying about the alarm going off?"

"If we trigger it by opening the door or something, the police could come and find us . . . and . . ." I could see that

Austin was starting to lose confidence as Zandy continued to glare at him.

She sighed in exasperation. "That alarm's been broken for years. It kept going off during the very first play I was in, back when I was seven, and no one could figure out how to fix it. So they pulled the wires out. They're still there on the wall in a big knot."

"Are you sure?" Austin looked at the can of shaving cream and dropped his arm to his side.

I didn't have to ask. As soon as I heard her say it, I realized she must have known the alarm didn't work. That's what had given her the courage to come here in the first place.

"Mrs. Mac showed the whole cast where they were tied, so we wouldn't worry about the alarm starting up again when we were onstage. I still check them on opening nights." She looked a little embarrassed. "It's just a habit."

Even best friends have secrets they don't share. I didn't know Zandy did that. And she definitely didn't know I touched the picture of Romeo and Juliet before every performance.

Austin put the can in his jacket and pulled out a flashlight. "Flat house," he said, shoved his bike with ours in the shelter of the bushes, and led the way as we sloshed through the mud and rain to the far side of the building.

The flat house is a kind of shed built on the outside of the theater. It's only used to store old flats and leftovers from the shop, and it looks like it. It has the kind of door you'd expect to find on a shed—old wood boards with a big latch held by a padlock. No one who saw it would guess that inside was a door that opened directly to the scene shop.

Sheds aren't the kinds of places that have a porch or any kind of overhang. There was nothing to do but stand in the rain as Austin held his flashlight in his teeth and dialed the combination. But in a few seconds, Austin pulled the lock off the latch. He slipped it into his pocket before he opened the door, and we stepped inside.

We couldn't turn on a light, because someone outside might see it. We waited in the dark, dripping and listening, just in case there was an alarm we didn't know about.

When we didn't hear anything, Austin turned his flashlight back on. He kept the beam turned down, shielding it with his hand. We moved slowly across the concrete floor, trying to avoid the jumble of old flats poking out unevenly into the narrow aisle, the pieces of lumber leaning against the wall, and the piles of leftover building materials everywhere. Austin had just opened the door that led to the shop when there was an enormous crash. Zandy had knocked over a couple of empty paint cans.

The racket made us all freeze momentarily until Austin finally motioned us on with his flashlight. But Zandy wasn't moving. She clutched my arm, hard. "Beth, we need to get out of here. Now."

I put my other arm around her and whispered fiercely in her ear, "The eviction begins tomorrow morning. Unless we find this bracelet tonight, we're not going to be doing any more plays here. Ever."

And your dad won't have any reason to come see you. I didn't have to say that. I knew Zandy was thinking it.

She took a deep breath, dropped my arm, and started walking.

The flashlight got us through the shop. Then it was easy. The ghost light lit our way across the stage. The stair railings, with the help of the flashlight, led us down to the basement and to the door of the costume room.

The three of us went straight to the jewelry cabinet. Zandy pulled out the center drawer. Austin shone the light over the neat rows of necklaces and bracelets, tiaras and rings. Zandy's magic wand glittered in the front. Huge jewels sparkled white, yellow, red, purple, and blue as the light hit them. They looked splendid—theatrical and absolutely fake. Nothing at all like the real diamonds in Mrs. Fredericks's bracelet.

We searched the jewelry drawers not being used in our play; first the bracelets, then the necklaces, and finally the drawer marked MISSALANEOUS. Some third grader must have written the label for it years ago. It used to make me smile whenever I saw it, but none of us were smiling now.

We closed the last drawer empty-handed then looked through each one once more.

"It's not here," said Zandy. "Let's go."

She started to walk toward the hallway, but I couldn't accept defeat that easily. I took the flashlight from Austin and ran the light over the whole room, just in case.

Suddenly I saw a gleam on the floor near the windows.

"Look." I kept the flashlight steady and started toward it, weaving my way around the cutting table and along the row of sewing machines. Austin and Zandy followed close behind.

The gleam got brighter as we got nearer. There, in the corner against the wall, shining in the light, was a pool of water. It grew slightly bigger as we watched.

"It's flooding," Austin said. "That water is seeping up from the ground through the concrete."

"What can we do?" I asked, watching the water grow larger.

"There's an old sump pump in the scene shop," he said. "It should take care of it."

"Why isn't it working?" I hissed.

"It only works if you turn it on. I'll find the switch when we get back to the shop."

I handed him the flashlight and we followed him out the door, up the stairs, and to the stage.

The ghost light had gone out.

"Is someone here?" Zandy sounded absolutely terrified.

"We left the door unlocked." I was scared, too. So scared I didn't even think of how unlucky it was for the ghost light to be off.

But Austin had a techie's view of the problem. "The bulb must have burned out. Should I stop and fix it?"

"No!" said Zandy with a sound like a whispered scream.

I was getting worried about her. Thank goodness we would be outside and heading home any minute.

We stumbled across the stage and into the scene shop. We've all built sets and props there, but Austin knew it like the back of his hand. He found the switch to the sump pump before I'd gotten more than a couple of feet in the room.

"That's funny," he said after he'd given it a flip.

"What's funny?" demanded Zandy.

"Did you hear anything?" he asked.

"Did you?" Her voice was a squeak.

"We should have heard the motor turn on." He flipped the switch off and on a couple of times then stared at it, thinking. "Shoot," he said finally. "I bet I know what's going on."

He walked to the door and reached for the light switch to the room.

"No," Zandy begged.

But he turned it on. Absolutely nothing happened.

"The power's out," Austin said. "That's why the ghost light is off. And if someone doesn't get an electrical generator hooked up to that sump pump pretty quick, the basement of this theater's going to be underwater by morning."

"Do you know how to hook up a generator?" I asked.

"If I had one, I bet I could figure it out." He ran his hand through his hair. "But I don't. We need to get help."

Zandy started shaking her head. I think she was too scared to talk. To be honest, I wasn't feeling real courageous myself. If my parents found out where I was, I would be grounded for life. And after all this, we hadn't found the bracelet.

Austin was still concerned about the flooding. "If the water rises much further, the props and the costumes will be ruined," he said.

I suddenly remembered running my fingers over the jet beads on the cape I wore when I played Martha Cratchett in *A Christmas Carol*. I was tracing the intricate pattern on the black silk, wondering how many actors had worn it and what other plays it had been in, when Mrs. Lester had called me over to her.

"That cape is over one hundred years old," she had told me. "Look at the sewing on the inside, all done by hand."

I flipped it up and studied the tiny stitches. "I wonder who made it. And who owned it."

Mrs. Lester had reached over and felt the heavy silk. "The materials—this silk, the jet beads—were expensive, so the person must have been fairly wealthy. And since it's all black, it was probably worn by someone in mourning."

Less than twelve hours from now we were going to lose our theater. Would we be mourning the loss of our costume collection as well?

There was no choice. We had to get help. And we had to do it now.

"Who do we call?" I asked.

I could almost hear Austin's brain clicking. "In an emergency, call 911," he said. "There's a phone here in the shop." He paused for a moment. "Cross your fingers that it's still working. We won't have to say anything. We'd just call and leave the receiver off the hook. When the police come to check it out, they'll search the whole building and find the flooding."

"And we'll be long gone." It was a good plan. With any luck at all, we'd be home free by the time the police arrived.

But Zandy was still shaking her head. "I need to go now," she said. "My mother can't find out I did this."

"Go ahead, Zan," I said. "Austin and I can finish up." It wasn't fair to desert him after all he'd done to help us.

"We'll be right behind you." Austin pointed the flashlight toward the door to the flat house and she disappeared through it. Then he walked over to the phone and picked up the receiver.

"I've got a dial tone," he said, and started to punch in the number.

We both heard something fall.

Maybe Zandy kicked the paint cans again on her way out.

Or maybe somebody—or something—was inside the building with us.

We raced out of the shop, through the flat house, and back to our bikes. I've never run so fast in my life. Austin was right behind me.

Zandy's bike was gone. I jerked mine out of the bushes and tried to hop on the seat. By then, my hands were so wet I couldn't get a grip on the handlebars. I wiped them frantically on my jeans and jumped again. The rain on the bike's seat instantly soaked through my jeans.

I don't think there is anything as uncomfortable as cold, wet denim.

As soon as I started to pedal, the rain came down even harder, lashing out of the sky until every inch of my clothes were drenched.

Austin grabbed his bike, made a running start, and almost slipped off because his seat was so slick. We stuck our helmets on as we were riding out of the driveway.

We'd pedaled down the street for at least a block before I asked, "Did you finish dialing?"

Austin's helmet bobbed. "I got an operator, dropped the phone, and ran. Let's hope someone comes to check it out."

What will happen if they don't? I thought.

"I didn't lock the padlock," he added. "I just threw it on the ground."

We rode in silence through empty roads lined with dark houses and windblown trees. My bike skidded as I steered around a large limb lying in the middle of the street, but I regained my balance.

"Thanks," I called to Austin before I turned off at the next block.

The hair hanging out the back of my bike helmet was plastered to my neck. I shook my head but it didn't budge. The rain was slashing so hard against my face I could barely see.

I stowed my bike at the side of the house and climbed quietly into my bedroom through my open window. I didn't think it was possible to feel worse than I did at that moment.

And then I heard my father's voice from the chair at the other end of my room. "And just where have you been, young lady?"

Chapter Ten

When sorrows come, they come not single spies but in battalions!

Shakespeare's *Hamlet*

Parents have a lot to say when they find you sneaking into the house after midnight. And they keep saying it, over and over.

My mother must have said, "I can't believe you broke into the theater—in the middle of the night—all by yourself," at least ten times.

My father must have said, "I can't believe you were biking around town—in the middle of the night—all by yourself," at least twenty times.

They both said, "Do you realize you could have been killed?" a lot more.

Somehow I managed to keep Zandy and Austin out of it. I told my parents that I'd ridden to Zandy's house and thrown pebbles at her window, but she never woke up. I said that I had opened the padlock to the back door once when I was working in the shop and remembered the combination.

Yeah, I lied, but how could I tell on Zandy? It would kill her if her mother found out. And Austin? He had come out in the middle of the night to help us. Dragging them into this wouldn't help me one little bit. And the rest of the story was true.

As soon as I mentioned the flooding, my father called Mrs. Mac. He didn't have any trouble finding her number.

It was really, really embarrassing that he had to tell her I broke into the theater. It helped a little that Mrs. Mac said it was logical to search for the bracelet in the jewelry cabinet, so logical that she'd checked there the day before. She thanked my dad for calling and said she would take care of the water seeping inside immediately before it did any real damage.

At least I saved the basement from flooding.

But as soon as my dad hung up the phone, the questions started again.

"Why did you have to talk to Zandy in the middle of the night?" asked my mother. "You'd been with her almost all day."

"Why couldn't you wait until the morning?" asked my father.

This time I didn't have to lie.

"Because it's Monday! The morning could be too late." I knew my reason for sneaking out would start to make sense to them. "I overheard Mrs. Fredericks say she was going to tell her lawyer to begin evicting us today. I wanted to find her bracelet before they started moving all the theater's stuff onto the sidewalk. Just in case it made her change her mind."

That's when my dad buried his head in his hands and started to breathe in big noisy gulps, his shoulders shaking up and down.

A wave of guilt swept over me. Had what I'd done made him cry?

Then I looked over at him and realized he was *laughing* at me. Hard.

"I'm tired," he said, wiping his eyes with the back of his hand. "So *that's* why you snuck out? You wanted to stop the eviction proceedings before they began?"

I nodded sulkily. His voice had gone squeaky when he said "eviction proceedings" like he was trying not to laugh again.

"Well, it gives me no end of relief to know that my daughter is not in the habit of acting like a juvenile delinquent without great provocation. But if you had bothered to ask me, I could have told you that all Mrs. Fredericks can do to evict you from the theater is get her lawyer to write a letter saying she's not going to renew the lease and she expects the theater to be vacated when the lease expires."

A wave of relief shot over me. We had a few more months to pray for a miracle. The lease didn't expire until September.

My mom looked at me and yawned. "We'll finish this tomorrow. Dad and I have to decide your punishment and right now I'm so angry that grounding you for the next ten years sounds way too mild."

She picked up my wet jeans and held them out in front of her with distaste. "Next time you're worried about a legal matter, ask your father instead of Zandy. That way I'll get a lot more sleep."

Dad got up to go back to bed, too. "There seems to be a certain misplaced logic in your actions," he said. "But they were very dangerous and there have to be some serious consequences." His voice sounded strained, like he was fighting to smother another laugh.

He reached out to ruffle my hair as he headed for the door. "Still, I'll see if I can talk your mother into a reduced sentence," he added. "After all, Scooter, I'm a lawyer. I'm good at that kind of thing."

It was after 3:00 a.m. before I fell asleep.

My stomach was crawling with mice, vicious beasts that were trying to eat their way out from the inside. When I heard the alarm go off in the morning, I woke up with a small cry of pain. We had lost the theater.

The first thing I did was take the phone under my covers and call Zandy. I didn't even say hello when she answered, just whispered, "I got caught last night. They don't know about you. Don't say anything."

I heard her gasp as I hung up.

I got out of bed and opened the curtains to a day that was mocking me. Sunshine poured in the windows and a hundred flowers chose today to bloom. I don't own a beaded black cape, so I put on the closest thing I had to mourning clothes—a black T-shirt and a pair of black jeans.

R. J. was coming out of the bathroom as I started down the hallway to the kitchen.

He looked worried. "What happened last night? I kept waking up hearing people talking."

"Didn't Mom and Dad say anything?"

"No, but they're really upset about something."

When you're sneaking out at night, you never think about how hard it's going to be to explain it to your little brother.

"I did something really dumb last night." I bent over and looked at his face to make sure he was taking this seriously. His eyes were staring straight into mine, his mouth open slightly. "I snuck out and rode my bike over to the theater to check something."

R. J. gave a little gasp.

"Mom and Dad caught me when I came home."

R. J. looked as shocked as I hoped he would—I never want him to make the same mistake I did. "What are they going to do to you?"

"I don't know yet."

I didn't know and I didn't care. Whatever they decided didn't matter. Our theater was closing, and I didn't think anything worse could ever happen to me.

It really helped that R. J. gave me a quick hug.

I got to school so late, I didn't get a chance to talk to Zandy until the first break.

We headed for the knobby old pepper tree at the back of the playing field where we go when we want to be alone. Poor Zan. She looked so guilty. When we reached the tree, she didn't say a word, just turned and ran a fingernail down the cracks in the trunk.

"My dad caught me climbing in the window last night," I said.

"Did you tell him about me?" Zandy half-whispered the question.

"No. I told you that when I called. What good would it do to get you in trouble?"

"Thank you," she said.

Then I told her the whole story of what happened, with as many details as I could remember. And sure enough, as soon as I was done, Zan asked again, "Are you sure no one knows about me?"

"I told you. Everyone thinks I was riding around town all by myself."

"Thanks. A lot." Zandy pulled one of the long pink strands of dried peppercorns off the tree and rubbed it between her hands. The puffy pink shells around each corn dissolved into dust. "What are your parents going to do to you?" she asked as she dropped the dark wrinkled corns one by one through her fingers.

I smelled the pepper and yawned.

"They grounded me for two weeks." Thanks to my dad. He is a very good lawyer.

"What about *Cinderella!?*" asked Zandy. "There are still four more performances."

"My grounding starts next Monday. My parents said they didn't want my punishment to hurt anyone else. So I get to finish the play. But I can't go to the cast party. And I have to apologize to Mrs. Mac."

"You're lucky," said Zandy, smiling a little. "My mom would have grounded me until I was thirty."

"Lucky? Starting next Monday, it's straight home after school, no friends, no phone, no texting, no email, no exceptions." I did a pretty good imitation of my mother's voice, but secretly I agreed with Zandy. I thought I was getting off pretty easy, too, except for having to face Mrs. Mac.

I rode to the theater alone after school the next day. The closer I got, the slower I pedaled. I was so ashamed of what I'd done.

I locked my bike to the rack then unlocked it and locked it again just to be sure it had clicked shut. I stopped to tie my shoe and rearranged the books in my back pack. But no matter how long I delayed, I finally arrived at the door to Mrs. Mac's office. It was open, of course, and she saw me before I could knock. I took a deep breath as I stepped inside, ready to begin my apology.

But Mrs. Mac spoke first. "Beth, everyone here owes you our deepest thanks for discovering the theater was flooding. Because of you, I was able to get a team in to pump out the water before it caused any damage."

I was so surprised I just stood there, mouth open, trying to grasp what was happening.

"The last time the basement flooded, we had to close the theater for three months. We lost half the costume collection and most of our props. You saved us from another disaster."

But I knew I had not played the heroine in this story. I took a breath and said, "I need to apologize for breaking in to the theater."

"Of course you do," Mrs. Mac agreed. "While your father assured me you did it with the best of intentions, it was wrong, and I want you to tell me you'll never do it again."

I shook my head back and forth. "I'll never do it again."

"Good." She paused as if searching for the best way to phrase her next comment. "How have your parents handled this?"

"I'm grounded for two weeks, but it won't start until after *Cinderella!* closes."

She smiled. "You have very considerate parents. It's good of them to think of everyone who are depending on you in this play."

I don't know if she meant for me to think about how close I'd come to letting everyone down, but if she did, it worked. I felt selfish.

"One more question," she said. "How did you get the door open?"

"I had to open the padlock once when I was working in the shop and I remembered the combination." It was so close to the truth. I couldn't mention Austin.

Mrs. Mac picked up a pencil and jotted a note on her desk. "Time to change the locks on that door," she muttered. "I doubt you're the only one who's memorized the combination." Then she looked up and pointed her pencil at me. "You're forgiven. I'll see you Thursday at the performance. "

I ran into Austin as I entered the lobby.

"Chuck Peterson asked me to come in to help dry up the damp places in the basement," he said. "I hear you were the *one* who caught the flooding."

"Don't tell anyone, but I rode over here *by myself* late at night and got into the theater."

"How did you do that?"

"I remembered the combination to the padlock. I just told Mrs. Mac. She's going to change the locks."

"Thank you," said Austin as he walked away toward the basement door.

Seeing Mrs. Mac wasn't so hard, I thought as I rode home. I bet the two weeks I'm grounded will just fly by. Zandy was right. I was pretty lucky when my parents decided how to punish me.

It wasn't until Saturday, the last night of the play, that I realized just how badly my punishment was going to hurt.

🎭

I always wear my grubbiest clothes to the final performance because we strike the set right after each play ends. We bow, the curtain comes down, the costumes and makeup come off, we get into our grubbies, and we start to work.

Our first job is to return our costumes to Mrs. Lester. She was stationed in the lobby, checking off each piece and putting them in the big cardboard boxes that go to the cleaners.

I was standing in line behind one of the Duchesses, holding my Cat's head, suit, and mittens, when I remembered the blue gown with the dripping pearls I'd worn for that one fateful performance.

"I already turned in the Duchess costume," I told her. "I left it to be mended the night I wore it."

Mrs. Lester looked down at her list. "Popped that in the dry cleaning box as soon as it was fixed. Now, off you go." She reached past me for the Frog's flippers another kid was holding.

I headed to the stage to tear down the tree outside Prince Charming's castle. We build new trees for almost every show because trees take so much room to store and are really easy to make. I'd taken off all the branches and was just starting to unwrap the burlap on the trunk when Mrs. Mac walked into the house and went straight to the seat she sits in when she's directing. We rarely see her during strike. Chuck Peterson is in charge then. But Mrs. Mac stood there, eighth row center, until she had our attention.

Almost everyone was onstage taking something apart. I don't think Mrs. Mac's ever made an announcement during strike before. That should have tipped us off that this was going to be serious, but we were all laughing and kidding around with that happy/sad feeling everyone gets at the end of a successful run.

She cleared her throat and we slowly stopped everything we were doing to listen to her.

"I'm very sorry to tell you that we will be losing the lease to this theater in a few months," Mrs. Mac said rather matter-of-factly.

Her announcement came as a shock to most of the kids.

"What? Why?" A few kids called out, but Mrs. Mac raised her hand and, in a few seconds, the silence in the theater was total. You probably could have heard a pin drop, if anyone had a pin, and if they could have relaxed their hands enough to let anything fall. One of the smallest Mice moved closer to Emily, who put an arm around her shoulder.

"Mrs. Marguerite Fredericks, who came to the opening night of your play, is the new owner of this building, and she has decided to use this space for an adult theater company. Our lease will expire in about five months."

"Did she ever find her bracelet?" Kwame Prentice, who played the King, called out.

"Not to my knowledge," said Mrs. Mac and went right back to the main point. "It will take us at least three months to move out of the theater."

I could feel drops of sweat tickling their way down the middle of my spine. I bit my lip and listened with everyone else.

"For that reason, we will not be able to schedule any plays during the summer. We are investigating whether we can find a stage to rent for an occasional production down the road. I hope the Oakfield Children's Theater will go on in some form, even without this building."

Mrs. Mac paused and looked at our despondent faces. Then she raised her voice. "But I'm mounting another play in this theater no matter what."

I think Emily started to clap first.

In a second, everyone was applauding. Cast and crew, we all gave Mrs. Mac a standing ovation from the stage, to thank her for that play and for all the plays she'd directed. Somehow, our clapping turned into a chant: "What-play-what-play-what-play."

She laughed and held up her hand. "I want to end our productions in this theater with the same play the theater opened with fifty years ago—*Romeo and Juliet*."

Romeo and Juliet!

There was a buzz of excitement, especially among the high school kids. They always get all the parts in Shakespearian plays.

But anyone can audition. And for the few minutes that I would be standing onstage and reading Juliet's lines during that audition, I'd be playing Juliet.

"As you know, the theater is always dark for two weeks between each play," Mrs. Mac continued.

I grinned. I wouldn't miss the auditions. I was only grounded for two weeks after today.

I sent up a quick private prayer: "Please, God, let this not be our last play. Help us save the theater." I was praying with such concentration, I almost missed what Mrs. Mac said next.

"But because we have so little time, I'm scheduling auditions for this Tuesday."

I don't cry very much and never in public. There was no way I was going to start now. Just to make sure, I walked off the stage, into the wings, and started to climb. Zandy found me about ten minutes later, curled up in one corner of the catwalk.

She sat down next to me and wrapped her arms around her knees.

"The high school kids get almost all the Shakespearian parts," she said.

"I know."

"I'm not auditioning for this play," said Zandy. "I'm just signing up for crew."

"Why not?"

"I'm not that good of an actress."

"You get better parts than I do."

"Only in musicals. I've always gotten small roles when I'm not singing. Maybe we can crew together this time," she said. She looked down on the stage, where the strike continued in a buzz of despair and excitement. "How about volunteering for props with me, E-lizzy-beth? Props always needs at least two people. And we'd get to see the play every night."

"You really don't want to audition?"

"If I got a part, I'd have to spend hours and hours memorizing Shakespeare," she said with a mock shudder.

How could someone as smart as Zandy feel that way? Shakespeare's writing was so beautiful—how could she not want the chance to work with it?

I know I did, more than I've wanted anything else in my life.

But how would I persuade my parents to let me audition?

That evening, it was R. J.'s turn to clear the table after dinner, and when he took the last of the plates into the kitchen, I told my parents that Mrs. Fredericks was closing the Children's Theater for good.

"What a shame," said my mother. She reached over and took my hand. "It was such a special place for you. For all of us—the audience, too."

My dad reacted like a lawyer. "What's the City Council's reaction to this? That theater's right in the middle of a public park. What else could it possibly be used for?"

"An adult theater."

My mother squeezed my hand.

My dad looked grave.

It was the perfect moment.

"*Romeo and Juliet* will be our last play," I said quietly. "Is there any way I could have just one day off my grounding to go to auditions on Tuesday?"

My parents looked at each other.

I held my breath.

And R. J. came in and asked if we had any more dishwasher soap.

By the time my mother came back from the kitchen, the mood was gone.

"If you auditioned and got called back, wouldn't you need to go to callbacks the next day?" asked my mother.

I nodded, slowly. I'd sort of hoped they wouldn't ask about the next step.

My father looked over at my mom with approval and turned back to me. "So far you would need two days off from your grounding," he said. "And when would rehearsals start?"

"Next Saturday," I said, even more quietly.

"And they'd run about six weeks."

I nodded again.

"So you're asking for a six-week-and-two-day respite from a two-week grounding?" he asked.

"You do realize that this punishment is for very serious misbehavior?" said my mother.

I looked down at the table and nodded one last time. I knew what their answer was going to be:

Straight home after school, no friends, no phone, no texting, no email, no exceptions.

CHAPTER ELEVEN

Read on this book,
That show of such an exercise may colour
Your loneliness.

Shakespeare's *Hamlet*

Two weeks is fourteen days—only 336 hours—but it seems like two years when you're stuck in your bedroom every day after school. When you're grounded by *my* parents, you go to your room and close the door. You don't get to watch TV or listen to the radio or use the computer.

School wasn't much better.

Everyone kept talking about the theater closing and the last play. All my friends asked me about it, until I told them I couldn't go to the auditions because I was grounded. Then no one talked about it in front of me. But whenever I walked up to a group of my friends, their conversation suddenly stopped and they all looked uncomfortable.

I wasn't a part of anything anymore.

Tuesday afternoon was the worst.

I came home from school and went straight to my room. My clock radio read 3:45 p.m.

Auditions started in fifteen minutes.

I felt very sorry for myself sitting there on my bed. I tried to hate my parents, but I couldn't. It was my fault I was grounded, and I knew it.

I started to pace back and forth between my bookcase and my closet. I wanted to be onstage reading those lines so bad!

And then I started wondering what lines they would be.

I have a whole shelf of plays in my bookcase, mostly ones I've been in, but there's also *The Complete Works of William Shakespeare*. My mom used it when she was in college. The book moved into my room after Mom and I saw *A Midsummer Night's Dream*. I loved the play so much I asked her where I could find a copy. She dug out the *Complete Works* so I could read it for myself.

I've read a couple of the plays. It's always easier to read one of them after you've seen it performed. I've even memorized some of my favorite lines.

My pacing slowed as I reached the bookcase again. I stopped, pulled the *Complete Works* from the shelf, and turned to *Romeo and Juliet*. As I read, I tried to figure out which scenes Mrs. Mac would choose for the audition.

Romeo and Juliet has a really clear plot. Romeo crashes Juliet's party where they meet and fall in love. The problem is their families hate each other. That's why she says, "Wherefore art thou Romeo?" in the famous scene on the balcony. She's not looking for him, like a lot of people think when they hear it; she's complaining about who he's related to.

I leaned what it meant in my drama class last year. Our teacher, Mr. Shelton, asked us to accent different words in that line to see how many different meanings we could get from it. We tried saying the words every which way, and almost all of us were convinced Juliet was searching for Romeo. Then Mr. Shelton passed out the rest of Juliet's speech. All we had to do was read the next line—"Deny thy father and refuse thy name," followed closely by "'Tis but thy name that is my enemy"—and it became pretty obvious that the question was *who* he was, not *where* he was. It was also pretty obvious that you need to read the whole speech before you can figure out how to say each line.

If I were directing, I'd probably have my final candidates for Romeo and Juliet read that scene during the auditions. It's one of the few times they talk to each other. But first, I'd have the girls read a scene with all the dialogue between women. Maybe the scene where the Nurse tells Juliet that Friar Lawrence will marry her and Romeo in secret.

I was so absorbed in reading the scenes that I was shocked when R. J. knocked on my door. The time had gone by so fast, I had no idea it was dinner time already. Maybe being grounded wouldn't be that hard.

That evening, I tried to figure out the scene the boys would be reading. It was harder to decide. By the time I turned off my light, I had read the play twice.

I was wrong. Being grounded got harder every day. I kept going back to *Romeo and Juliet*. There wasn't much else to do and it helped me imagine what was happening at the theater.

I would have gone crazy if Zandy hadn't filled me in at school on what was happening with the play. I was right about what scenes the girls were reading. But not the boys.

By the end of the first week, I had read the play through five times and memorized most of Juliet's part. It was easy; she kept talking about being locked up.

Boy, could I relate to that.

I quoted a couple of her lines with great emotion every time I went back to my room. The first night I got up from the table, gripped the back of my chair, bowed my head, and said with great sadness:

O, shut the door, and when thou hast done so,
Come weep with me; past hope, past cure, past help!

My parents just rolled their eyes when they heard me. R. J. stuck his fingers in his ears. I didn't get any sympathy.

And neither did Juliet. Thirteen was old enough to get married back then, and her father decided to marry her off. He didn't know she was already married to Romeo. She begged her parents not to make her do it, but they wouldn't listen.

To escape, Juliet was going to take a drug that would make her appear dead. After her funeral, Romeo was going to rescue her from her family's mausoleum so they could run away together. When Juliet talked about being locked up, it was in a windowless stone building with the rotting bodies of her ancestors.

Shall I not then be stifled in the vault,
To whose foul mouth no healthsome air breathes in

I quoted that at the end of dinner the next night, just before I returned to my room.

R. J. looked at me like he thought I was nuts, and my parents just burst into laughter as I trudged down the hall.

The next night, I stopped when I reached the hallway, turned back toward the table, and held out a melancholy arm toward my mother as I said:

Is there no pity sitting in the clouds,
That sees into the bottom of my grief?
O, sweet my mother, cast me not away!

That didn't work the way I intended.

My dad looked at my mom and said, "You know I wouldn't want to push her, but don't you think Beth's a natural for law school? With her memory and her ability to speak in public, I can't think of another career that would suit her better."

Great.

From Juliet to Portia in just one quote.

Two weeks is a long, long time.

The second week I was grounded, Zandy tried to tell me the bad news in our regular spot under the pepper tree. "I signed us both up for crew," she said.

"At least we'll get to work on *Romeo and Juliet* together," I said. "It's great. I've read it seven times now."

"Seven times!"

"Reading it 'hast comforted me marvelous much.'"

"I'll bet," Zandy said. She was rolling peppercorns in her hand again and blowing away the pink shells. That usually means she's worrying about something.

I waited.

"Austin's going to be the stage manager. Scott Stirling's going to be his assistant."

I knew Scott. He was a junior in high school. He'd been the stage manager for the *Wizard of Oz* and *Oliver!* He was as good as Austin, if not better. It would be super working backstage with the two of them.

"Just another week and I'll be over there crewing with you," I said with a half smile.

Then Zandy blurted out what was worrying her: "Chuck Peterson said no one can work backstage if they don't turn up for the ten a.m. crew meeting on Saturday."

"Why?"

I'd never heard of anyone who volunteered to crew being turned down. You might not get the job you wanted most, but they always found something that needed doing. I was sure I could get around that one and I said so.

Zandy looked down at the peppercorns in her hand. "There's so many kids working backstage, we're tripping over each other. Everyone wants to be part of this play because it's the last one."

I felt a rush of jealousy. Zandy wouldn't be working on the play if I hadn't taken all the blame, but I pushed the thought to the back of my mind. The important thing I needed to concentrate on was finding a job, any job. There was no way I wasn't going to be a part of this production.

"If I can't crew, I'll just usher every night."

Zandy plucked a peppercorn out of her palm and threw it at the tree. "All the usher slots filled Wednesday."

That night, my mom wandered into my room with a copy of the *San Francisco Chronicle* in her hand.

"Look what I found," she said. "A picture of . . ." She stopped and read the caption again. "Marguerite Fredericks. She was at the theater last week. Mrs. Mac introduced her before the play began. She's related to Lucille Bow somehow."

Mom looked at me to see if I knew who she was talking about.

I knew who she was talking about all right.

"Mrs. Fredericks must really like theater," she said. "This picture was taken at a reception for a very famous director, Quinn Whitaker."

I made my face go blank.

My mother started to explain, as if I didn't know who she meant. "He was the director of that Winter Shakespeare Festival in Canada. The one that was written up in the papers."

When I still didn't react, her voice became insistent. "Beth, I know you've heard of Quinn Whitaker."

"Didn't his theater burn down recently?" It hurt to ask.

"Right! Even losing his theater made international news." She sounded pleased that I had made the connection. "You can read about it yourself."

She put the newspaper down on my bed as she left. I stared at it as though she had just left a live cobra in my room. Finally, I reached over and picked it up. There was a picture of Mrs. Fredericks and a man with a shock of dark curls standing together and talking. I read the caption under the picture very carefully:

Quinn Whitaker and Marguerite Fredericks chat at a reception honoring outstanding accomplishments in the arts. Whitaker was named Most Innovative Director for his outdoor staging of Shakespeare's The Winter's Tale *on a frozen lake after his theater was destroyed by fire. Whitaker is looking for a new facility and, when questioned, said he might consider moving his award-winning theater company to the United States if the right location became available.*

I threw the paper in the wastebasket and flopped down on my bed. I picked up *Romeo and Juliet* and put it right back down. I couldn't read.

What else could she do with a 248-seat theater in a public park?

That would make a good vocal exercise. By accenting different words, how many different meanings would you give that phrase?

The second Saturday I was grounded was the worst day of my life. No school, no church, nothing but the desolation of my room. When my clock flashed 10:00 a.m., I knew the mandatory crew meeting had started. My last chance to be part of a production at the Oakfield Children's Theater was gone. I couldn't imagine what my life would be like without it.

The hours crawled by. I was lying on my bed, bored with everything, most of all with my own company, when I heard a faint scratching sound near my door. I went to investigate and found a small plastic army man lying on the floor. As I reached down to pick it up, another slid slowly under the door to join him.

R. J. had sent his army men on a mission to make me feel better. We spent an hour talking through the crack beneath my door.

"Is the theater really going to close?" he asked.

"Looks like it."

"What will you do?"

I wanted to make him feel better so I answered as positively as I could.

"I'll be in high school in a year and a half. I can act in plays there."

"A year's a really long time."

Eight-year-olds are not good at waiting. Who am I kidding? Twelve-year-olds think a year's a really long time, too, especially if it's a year without acting.

"While I'm waiting, I'll become a triple threat."

Both R. J. and the army men liked the sound of that. I heard a soft laugh and three more green plastic figures appeared under the door.

"Here comes a triple threat," he said. Then there was a long pause, followed by, "What's a triple threat?"

"Someone who can act and sing and dance. I'll start taking dance classes and vocal lessons and you'll be stuck coming to recitals instead of plays."

The exaggerated groans that came from the other side of the door were just what I hoped to hear.

The funny thing about trying to make someone else feel better is you start feeling better yourself.

After the Children's Theater closed, I would keep on training. There were dance studios and vocal coaches in town. I would take the train to San Francisco and study there. When I turned sixteen, I would drive to rehearsals.

I kept thinking of what Mrs. Mac said: "What's silly is to worry about something without doing anything about it."

I couldn't use the Internet, but I got out the phone book and made a list of who to call about lessons when I could finally use the phone again.

I stared at my list, biting the end of my pen, and then started another one. There were only two items on the second list.

When my two weeks were finally up, I headed straight from school to the theater. It was the first task on that second list. I wanted to work on *Romeo and Juliet* and the only way

I could figure out how to do it was to get special permission from Mrs. Mac.

I didn't ask Zandy to come with me; this time I had to see Mrs. Mac alone.

Her door was open, but so much depended on the next few minutes it was hard to find the courage to knock on it. The only thing harder would be to give up and go home.

I knocked.

"Beth, how can I help you?" Mrs. Mac asked, looking up from the costume sketches she was studying,

"I'd like to crew for *Romeo and Juliet*," I said. "But since I've been grounded for the last two weeks I missed the crew meeting on Saturday. Is there any way I can still help backstage?"

It sounded good. Okay, I had written it out, memorized it in school that day, and rehearsed it all the way to the theater. I was proud I got up the nerve to say it.

Mrs. Mac frowned. "I'm sorry," she said. "But you know the rules. If you miss a rehearsal or a crew meeting for any reason but illness, you can't work on the play."

"There's nothing I can do?" My voice slowed down with each word.

"Come and see the play. The audience is a vital part of the theater, too. You know that."

I bit my lip and looked down at the floor, trying to think of something else to say. A muffled yell and the sudden sound of clashing metal sounded through the room. My head jerked up, and I bit down so hard I could taste blood.

"What's that?" I asked as the metallic clash, accompanied by heart-wrenching shrieks and snarls, rang out again and again.

Mrs. Mac looked back down at the sketches on her desk and sighed. "Swords. The specialist in stage fighting is going to be working in the rehearsal room every afternoon until they're ready to go onstage. And I'm going to need to work with the door closed with all that going on. Would you . . . ?"

She left the request unspoken but it was a clear signal that it was time for me to go.

"Shut the door?" I asked, and she nodded.

I was shutting off part of my life with the closing of that door. I'd never be in another play at the Children's Theater. The sound of the swords clanging against each other was much louder near the hallway, certainly loud enough to cover my voice as I reached for the handle.

"'O, shut the door, and when thou hast done so, Come weep with me; past hope, past cure, past help!'" Just as I started speaking, there was a muffled shout and all the noise stopped. My voice came out much louder than I expected.

"What?" Mrs. Mac's head popped up and her voice was startled. "What did you say?"

"It's just one of Juliet's lines," I said, leaning on the doorknob. "I read *Romeo and Juliet* about ten times when I was grounded."

Mrs. Mac was staring at me so hard that I felt I had to explain more.

"Two weeks is a very long time to be. . . 'stifled in the vault, To whose foul mouth no healthsome air breathes in.'"

"And you spent that time . . . ?" Mrs. Mac was using the same brisk tone that she uses when she directs, when she's trying to get someone to do more with a line, to try a different direction.

"I memorized a lot of Juliet's speeches."

"Why?"

How could I answer a question like that? "It comforted me."

"How much?"

"'Marvelous much.'"

We were playing a word game but I didn't know the rules. I thought I was giving the right answers by quoting Juliet's lines, but Mrs. Mac suddenly changed the playing field. She glanced down at the costume sketches in front of her.

"How tall are you?"

"Five-foot-two."

She looked up, staring like she was running through everything she knew about me.

"Emily Chang is playing Juliet," she said. "I'm having a problem casting her understudy because Emily's so petite and her understudy needs to be able to wear her costume."

I nodded. I was afraid to say anything. What if Mrs. Mac's thoughts weren't going where mine were?

"Scheduling is an even bigger concern," she went on. "Since I moved up the dates for this play, our rehearsals conflict with the high school's SAT exams. I'm having trouble finding an actor who wants to take the time from her studies to learn a major Shakespearean part for a role as an understudy. Especially since Emily is playing Juliet . . ."

Mrs. Mac didn't have to say any more. Everyone knew that Emily would be onstage for every performance unless she really did break a leg. And even then she'd probably find a pair of crutches in the prop room and go on anyway.

Mrs. Mac pulled a pencil out of her hair and tapped the eraser lightly on her desk, still staring at me. "It seems your parents gave you a gift of time and you used it well." She gave a final decisive tap and smiled. "Would you like to understudy Juliet?"

"Yes. Of course."

Would I like to be a part of the last play at the Oakfield Children's Theater?

Yes.

Would I like to play Juliet? Would I like to have my biggest dream come true?

Yes. Yes. Yes.

"You've just been given the part, so technically you haven't missed any rehearsals," said Mrs. Mac. "Sit in the house and watch whenever you can and try to learn her blocking."

I finally thought of something else to say. "Thank you. Thank you so much."

She pulled a pencil out of her hair and glanced at the costume sketches again, but she had one more thing to say. "Emily is seventeen now, and you're . . . ?" She paused for me to answer.

"Almost twelve and three-quarters."

Mrs. Mac smiled again. "Almost thirteen. Juliet's age. It will be very interesting to see the difference in how you and Emily play the character. You've grown as an actress in the last year. I'm looking forward to working with you on this role, even if it's just at the one understudy rehearsal."

We both knew there wasn't a chance I'd get onstage for anything else, but I didn't care. I was a going to be part of the last play at my theater. I was playing Juliet. What more could I ask for?

Chapter Twelve

Like a dull actor now,
I have forgot my part

Shakespeare's *Coriolanus*

I flew down the street, pumping my bicycle harder than I ever had before. I was playing Juliet!

What if I hadn't gotten up the courage to ask Mrs. Mac to be part of the play? My bike jerked to the side. Just thinking about it made me lose my balance.

Now I had to find enough courage to talk to my parents. The second item on my list. And the hardest.

I'd been trying to figure out why Juliet didn't tell her parents she was already married when her father ordered her to marry someone else. And I think I understood.

Juliet knew her father would be angry and disappointed. She didn't want to face hurting him so badly. But she died because she kept her marriage a secret. And she hurt him even more. Her poor parents were left to find her lifeless body in the family tomb. Wouldn't they rather have learned the truth than lost their daughter?

It was time to tell my father the truth—time to tell him I wanted to become an actor.

I slowed my bike and coasted for a while, planning how to explain my decision. I'd wait till after dinner, just before we left the dining room table. I'd tell my parents I was going to understudy Juliet. I would be clear and businesslike. My dad would like that.

But when I got home and saw my mom through the kitchen window, I threw my bike down on the ground and ran into the house screaming, "I got in! I got in! I got in!"

She'd heard it before.

"So the grounding didn't matter after all?" Mom asked. She sounded genuinely happy for me.

"It did matter," I said. "I only got in because I'm good."

"Elizabeth, that sounds very conceited," said my dad.

He was on the other side of the kitchen, chopping broccoli with his Chinese cleaver.

"I had to know I'm good before I could tell you this," I said and took a deep breath. "I want to be an actor when I grow up."

Thownk! went the cleaver.

"Actors don't make enough money to live on," said my father.

"Some do," I said.

"Really, Beth?" said my mother, "Just because Mrs. Mac was kind enough to add in a part for you, you suddenly decide to make acting your career?"

"I'm understudying Juliet," I said.

Thwonk! went the cleaver.

We talked in the kitchen and we talked during dinner. We sat around the table long after R. J. got up to play in his room.

And we struck a deal. If the theater closed, my parents would let me study acting in San Francisco when I turned sixteen.

"If you're still interested then," my father kept repeating.

In the meantime, they would pay half for vocal lessons and half for dance lessons, but only if I looked into other professions, as well.

"Acting is such a gamble," said my mother. "You have to have some other way to earn enough money to buy food."

"And to pay your rent," added my father, brushing a few stray grains of salt into a neat pile on the tablecloth. "I suppose you know that I've always hoped you'd become a lawyer."

My mother and I both smiled at each other.

"You tell me almost every day," I said, still smiling.

He looked up from the salt pile. "It's a job you can support yourself with. What do you think about working at my office after school? You could earn the money you'll need for your lessons and you'd also learn something about the law."

"I'd really like that," I said.

I would. That experience could be very useful. I might play Portia someday. And there are all those TV shows about lawyers.

I loved working on the role of Juliet. Since Mrs. Mac had told me she didn't expect me to copy what Emily was doing, I felt free to create my own version of the character.

On Sunday, Zandy came over and helped me work on the blocking in my bedroom. She read all the parts—except Juliet—as I walked through the role and tried to remember where to move and when.

I held up my pencil jar and said, "Romeo, I come! This do I drink to thee," and almost stabbed myself in the eye as I mimed taking a drink of poison.

I walked three steps to my bed and fell on it, losing a pencil or two in the process.

"No," said Zandy. "The blocking's been changed. Now you hold up the vial, walk the three steps, then drink and fall." She eyed my pencil jar. "An obvious victim of lead poisoning."

Zandy knew the blocking better than I did. She was working the followspot and had a bird's eye view of the stage from the lighting booth at the back of the house. She'd watched the play from there all last week so she could learn where the actors were when she needed to follow them with the spotlight.

When we finished running through all the scenes I was in, we went to the kitchen for a glass of milk. I was scouting around to see if I could find any junk food to go with it when Zandy said, "I like your Juliet more than Emily's."

"You're a good friend, Zan," I said, feeling a little embarrassed and really pleased.

"Your Juliet is much dumber."

"You're a good friend, Zan," I said, feeling more embarrassed and a lot less pleased.

"You know what I mean. You're doing it deliberately. Your Juliet just rushes into dumb things," she said. "Emily's Juliet sounds very mature, like she's thinking things through, so I forget how stupid she is."

"You think Juliet's stupid?" I stopped rummaging for food and turned around to look at Zandy.

"Really, really dumb. And so's Romeo. They've known each other one day and they run off and get married. That's not smart."

"Well, no."

"Then, when Juliet's parents want to marry her to another guy, does she tell them she's married already?" Zandy was leaning against the counter, her hands on her hips. I was going to agree with her but she didn't wait for me to answer. "Not our Juliet. She turns to drugs."

"Not exactly," I started to protest.

But Zandy went right on. "She gets an unknown 'potion' that will knock her out so badly everyone will believe she's dead. Sounds like a drug to me. And does it occur to her that maybe her parents would rather hear she's married than find her dead? No, she never thinks ahead."

"She does." I'd read that play so many times, I could argue any point about Juliet's actions. "She's afraid that she'll wake up in her family tomb all alone with her rotting ancestors before Romeo gets there." I really liked the lines about being stifled in the family vault. "And she does wonder if maybe the potion in the vial is really poison . . ."

"And then she just swallows it down, not knowing what's in it." Zandy raised her glass of milk and looked at it in disgust. "That is really stupid."

"She got the potion from a priest."

"Would you trust a priest who secretly married a thirteen-year-old to her family's arch enemy?"

"I was trying to make Juliet look thirteen," I said.

Zandy looked a little startled. She took a sip of the milk.

"That must be why I like the way you play her. She's a dumb kid," she said finally. "She acts like we do."

This time I was a little startled. I'd tried to make Juliet act impulsively, like I saw some of the kids in my class act, but I thought Zandy and I were much more mature.

"Neither of us have snuck off to be married yet," I finally said.

"We snuck off to the theater in the middle of the night," said Zandy.

"That's different."

"Think that's not stupid? It was dangerous. We snatched at what we wanted without thinking, just like Juliet. And we lost the theater anyway."

Zandy paused and ran her finger around the rim of her glass. "I'm still trying to figure out how we can get Mrs. Fredericks to give it back to us."

Mrs. Fredericks's words started running through my head: *A children's theater isn't good enough. Not for him.*

I rinsed out my glass and put it in the sink. I wasn't hungry anymore.

Zandy put her glass in the sink next to mine. "I think our only chance to save the theater is to show Mrs. Fredericks what a great job we're doing with *Romeo and Juliet.*"

For a moment I felt a glimmer of hope. Maybe miracles could happen. This production was certainly turning into something very special.

Chuck Peterson had designed some incredible sets. The walls of Juliet's house looked like they were made of real stone. So did the family mausoleum with its line of stone tombs stretched across the stage. On top of each tomb, an actor playing a dead Capulet lay under a dusty gray veil. When the fog machine started and clouds of soft white smoke went billowing across the floor, the stage turned into a really scary place, full of death and sadness.

Mrs. Lester had pulled almost all the costumes from stock, and she'd found some magnificent ones—lots of velvets and brocades, slashed and laced like the portrait of the first Queen Elizabeth in *The Complete Works of William Shakespeare*. The lighting and music were just beginning to add their magic. And you could see the actors grow better from day to day. Everyone was working with a single purpose: to make this play the best one ever done at our theater. It looked like they were succeeding.

But it was still a children's production, still *not good enough*.

I sighed. "Mrs. Fredericks lives in New York. Do you think she'll even see it?"

Zandy grinned at me. "Mrs. Mac sent her two seats—fourth row center—and invited her to come on opening night."

"And . . . ?"

"She accepted."

I walked over to the old photograph hanging on the back wall of the lobby and glanced around casually to make sure no one else was nearby.

The teenage couple was still gazing into each other's eyes. I touched the last word of the first line on the brass plaque softly.

"Today," I said under my breath and headed for the dressing room.

I was playing Juliet.

Only once, only at an understudy rehearsal with no audience, but today the part was mine.

🎭

Understudy rehearsals are always disasters. Maybe because they're held at the end of the rehearsal period when everyone's tired and stressed. Maybe because everyone acting in them has never walked through the part before. Someone's always breaking up and laughing or drying up and forgetting their lines.

I wasn't worried. I was line perfect. I'd wanted to play Juliet for so long, I was going to make the most of my first chance with the role.

My mother once told me that "may you get what you wish" is an old Chinese curse. That never made sense to me before that rehearsal.

I only had seven lines in my first scene, but I knew it went well. You can feel it when you're doing a good job acting—your movement onstage flows naturally out of what you're saying; the other actors react to your cues better; you can hear the audience respond, even if it's just the director and a few curious cast members.

My second scene was the banquet where Romeo and Juliet meet and exchange their first kiss.

I considered myself an old hand at stage kisses. Jeffie Peabody and I kissed at the end of *Snow White and Rose Red* and had to hold it till the curtain fell. Jeffie and I were both nine at the time and dressed in bear suits. Last year, I'd kissed Graham Stewart repeatedly, and always on the correct beat of the music, when we were dancing jitterbugs in *The Wizard of Oz*.

But the understudy for Romeo was Christopher D'Angelo.

Christopher was a senior in high school. I'd never been in a play with him before, but I saw him play the lead in *High School Musical*. Half the high school girls had crushes on him.

Christopher did not kiss like Jeffie Peabody.

The first time Christopher kissed me, I blushed beet red and forgot my next line. Austin gave me the first word and I remembered the rest of the speech.

But I forgot my next line.

And the next.

I studied my lines furiously every minute I was offstage, but I kept drying up. And every time he had to feed me another line, Austin looked out from the wings as if he couldn't believe it was me. I even needed prompting in the famous balcony scene. The only line I managed to get through on my own was, "O Romeo, Romeo! wherefore art thou Romeo?"

You can feel it when you're doing a bad job acting—your movement onstage is awkward; the other actors don't react to your cues; and you can hear the audience twitching, even if it's just the director. I knew I was botching up the role, but I couldn't get it right.

We finally reached the last scene. I woke from my drugged coma, found Romeo dead, and managed to kiss him, stab myself, and still remember my lines. I felt the most enormous relief as I fell to the floor. I couldn't mess up anything else now.

I lay motionless, half-sprawled over Romeo's dead body, desperate for the play to end. I could feel the warmth of the spotlight that shone on us. Zandy was at the other end of it.

She must hate this part of the play, I thought. I could just hear her saying, "Romeo kills himself because he thinks Juliet's dead. He couldn't get a doctor to make sure? And then when Juliet wakes up and finds his body, she kills herself, too. Stupid! Stupid! Stupid!"

I wanted to giggle.

I tried to control it, laughing through my nose in a series of whimpers, my stomach heaving up and down, my eyes scrunched tightly together. Finally I stopped.

I opened my eyes a sliver to see if anyone had noticed and saw Christopher's eyes about eight inches away from mine, crinkling in silent laughter.

A large snort burst from my nose.

All the Capulets and Montagues gathered to mourn us, and all the dead Capulets lying veiled on their tombs broke up. Gales of laughter rang through the theater at the tragic end of Juliet and her Romeo.

If Mrs. Fredericks had seen this production, she'd have given the theater to the first flea circus that came along. And I wouldn't have blamed her.

CHAPTER THIRTEEN

But when her lips were ready for his pay,
He winks, and turns his lips another way.

Shakespeare's "Venus and Adonis"

I watched the last dress rehearsal from the audience. Emily was so good as Juliet. My eyes began to fill as she pleaded with her father not to make her marry someone else. I was crying as the scene ended with her passionate whisper: "If all else fail, myself have power to die."

The lights went out and I brushed the tears away, sniffing. Then from out of the darkness came a shout and a thud.

The lights came up immediately. Emily lay in a heap on the stage. The theater was silent except for an anguished "No!" from someone in a rear seat. It would have been me, if I'd been able to speak.

Everyone—Mrs. Mac, the closest crew members, the cast standing in the wings—rushed to her. I couldn't see anything through the crowd.

Was Emily hurt so badly I would have to take over her part?

I crossed all my fingers, pressing them together so hard it hurt, breathing, "No, no, no," under my breath. The future of our theater rested on Emily getting right back up.

And she tried.

She stood, took a wobbly step, then another, and looked down, a little bewildered. "I think I ripped my hem."

Mrs. Mac was watching Emily carefully. "Are you up to taking it to the costume shop to be fixed?"

We were all watching her.

Then Emily laughed and bounced up and down on her toes twice. "Don't worry. I'm fine." She kicked at the bottom of her gown, which was trailing on the floor. "Except for a droopy hem." She picked up the skirt in both hands. "I couldn't see the tape. I missed the bottom step and tripped on my dress."

Mrs. Mac continued to study Emily for a long moment, then smiled and nodded her head. Everyone went right back to work. The crew re-taped the step. Mrs. Mac talked to Chuck about putting someone backstage with a flashlight to illuminate the stairs. Emily headed to the costume shop.

And almost before I knew what I was doing, I slipped out of my seat and headed after her.

Holding up her skirts made Emily walk slower, and I'd almost caught up to her by the time she reached the door of the costume shop.

"You're really okay?" I called.

She turned and frowned at me. "Sorry to disappoint you," she said coolly. "I'm supposed to actually break my leg before you get my role."

She reached for the doorknob but I stuck my arm out and held the door shut, forcing her to look at me.

"You just scared me to death," I blurted out. "I had to be sure you're okay." My hand fell from the door. "You're doing such a great job as Juliet, you just had me in tears. The last thing I want is to go on in your place."

I didn't say, "Because we're all counting on your performance to persuade Mrs. Fredericks to give us back our theater and everyone will hate me if I blow it," but I'm pretty sure we both knew what I meant.

I bit my lip and looked down at the painted concrete floor. When I looked back up, Emily was smiling at me. She started to say something, but a guy doing props rushed by with a "Good luck tomorrow on the math test" as he passed.

Emily made a face and called after him. "Don't jinx it. We're in a theater here. How about 'break a leg'?"

He raised a hand in dismissal as he turned the corner.

"You've got a math test tomorrow?" Poor Emily. The same day as opening night.

She nodded. "Rotten timing, isn't it?" she said, as she opened the door to the shop. "At least it's in the morning. And I'm good at math."

School was a blur the next day. The only thing I remember was Ms. Davis calling my name at the start of creative writing.

"Elizabeth!"

When I got to her desk, she handed me a slip of green paper, obviously from the office. I opened it and found a message from my mother:

Mrs. Macintosh called. She wants you to go to the theater right after school. It's okay with me but be home for dinner.

I spent the whole period trying to figure out why Mrs. Mac wanted me.

By the time I had gotten my bike and was pumping my way down the street, I had narrowed it down to three possibilities. Best case: Mrs. Mac had found the bracelet. She wanted me to give it to Mrs. Fredericks so Mrs. Fredericks would remember my tour of the theater and decide to give the theater to us.

Okay, the logic was a little shaky on that one. That was the tour where Mrs. Fredericks found out I had been using a New York accent just like hers for its comic effect. The tour with that truly memorable cream cheese sandwich.

Next case: there was some extra work that Mrs. Mac needed help with, ironing some costumes or stapling some programs, and she knew she could depend on me. Good chance it's that one.

I turned onto the bike path through the park. There was a third case scenario: Emily was sick and I had to step in as understudy. I steered around a pothole and grinned. No worries there. Emily would crawl to the theater through a snowstorm even if she came down with the black plague.

I was still thinking about horrendous diseases that wouldn't faze Emily the least bit as I locked my wheel to the bike rack outside the theater. Maybe that's why I didn't come up with a fourth possibility.

After all, Emily's the one who's good at math.

Very, very good.

"Emily's in LA?"

I was standing in front of Mrs. Mac's desk, trying to make sense of what she had just told me.

"But Emily had a math test this morning. She couldn't have flown anywhere." I added the clincher, "She's good at math."

Mrs. Mac leaned back in her chair and smiled wryly. "Very good. She's been taking part in some math Olympics . . . Olympiad. Which I only learned about two hours ago, when she called and told me she'd taken a test this morning at UCLA and missed her flight home."

Mrs. Mac picked up a pencil and stuck it in her hair. There were at least three in there already. "You may need to play Juliet tonight."

I stopped breathing for a moment. Then shook my head. "Can't she get another flight?" It came out too loud.

Mrs. Mac flinched slightly. "It seems the Apple computer convention starts today, and all the flights between LA and San Francisco are sold out until nine o'clock tonight." She reached into her hair, grabbed a pencil, jiggled it up and down for a minute, then stuck it back. "She's on the wait list. She could still get back in time."

Yes! Of course she could. And there were other ways to get here.

"She could drive," I said. "She could rent a car."

"It would take at least eight hours to drive here." I was frantically doing the math when she added, "And car companies don't rent to teenagers."

Mrs. Mac pushed her chair back from her desk and stood up. "Don't worry," she said. "I really think Emily will get a flight in time, but until we know for sure, we need to assume you will have to step in."

Mrs. Mac would never have cast me as Emily's understudy if she thought there was the slightest chance I'd go on. But she did and I took the role. Neither of us could quit now.

"Of course," I said, my face frozen. What I wanted to say was, *I'm not good enough, I'll mess up the whole production and everyone will blame me for losing our theater. Especially me.*

"I've called an emergency rehearsal," said Mrs. Mac. "We'll only run the scenes Juliet is in." She looked at her watch. "Go get into her first costume. Zed should be here any minute."

I was extra careful as I stepped into Emily's gown. After all, I was just borrowing it for the afternoon. I was borrowing Emily's Romeo, too. In the understudy rehearsal, I'd been working with Christopher, along with the rest of the understudy cast, but now I needed to rehearse with the real Romeo, Zed Miller.

Just as I got to the wings, I saw him racing down the aisle. Zed's tall, and kind of cute, with chestnut brown hair and the happiest smile. He waved to Mrs. Mac and ran up the steps to the stage.

Zed and I have been in a lot of plays together. He's a junior in high school, almost four years older than me, but he's so funny and so nice to everyone that I've always felt he was one of my theater friends. I had to practice moving in Juliet's costumes, but Zed didn't need to change. He'd been rehearsing in his doublet and cloak for weeks.

Zed was still breathing deeply when he joined me. He put his arm around my shoulders and led me farther back into the wings.

"I saw the understudy rehearsal Tuesday," he said softly. "And I think it would help if we kissed before we go on-stage."

I couldn't meet his eyes. I looked down and nodded, embarrassed and ashamed.

And Zed bent down, took my face in both hands, tilted it up, and solemnly kissed me on the tip of my nose.

We went over our scenes together twice before the rest of the cast arrived, then we ran the other scenes I was in. My concentration was absolute. I did not forget one word. I did not laugh once.

I was perfectly wooden in each and every line.

Finally it was over. We all perched on the tombs in the Capulet's mausoleum while we listened to Mrs. Mac give the briefest of notes, mostly on when I should enter the stage during the party scene and where I should be at cur-tain call. She was just finishing when Chuck Peterson came out of the shop.

"Emily's on the phone," he said.

Mrs. Mac was only gone about two minutes. When she came back in, the theater became so quiet that we could hear her footsteps as we watched her walk down the aisle to the stage.

"Thank you all for coming to an extra rehearsal at the very last minute," she said. "It was very important that we held it. Emily has not gotten a flight, so Beth will be playing Juliet tonight." She paused for that to sink in before she added, "Hurry home for dinner. You're due back here in about an hour."

We left the stage quietly. Everyone looked as miserable as I felt.

Chapter Fourteen

*I pray you mar no more of my verses with reading them
ill-favouredly.*

Shakespeare's *As You Like It*

I glanced around casually to make sure no one else was in
the lobby before I walked over to the photograph hanging on the back wall. I looked one more time, then touched
the last word of the first line on the brass plaque.

"Tonight," I whispered.

Even on opening night, even with a play with a really large
cast, you can usually find somewhere to be alone. I went
into the prop room, sat down on a papier-mâché copy of
a Roman column, and thought of Juliet—as the gentle,

obedient daughter, as the flirt, as madly and dangerously in love.

And as a dumb thirteen-year-old. As quick to run off in the night to solve a problem as . . . as me. Zandy had been right: Juliet acted like we do. She was as reluctant to ask her parents for help as I was. As likely to change from happiness to despair as I was. Shakespeare had written the most wonderful character and I was going to play her. I was half excited and half scared silly.

"Beth Sondquist," I said to myself. "You are almost thirteen years old, and this is your thirteenth play . . ."

Whoa! Not the best line of thought. At least "13 Superstitions Every Theater Kid Should Know" doesn't say anything about the number thirteen being unlucky.

Time to get to the dressing room.

Whenever there's a sword fight in a play, the actors rehearse it before every single performance. All the girls in the cast were crowded into our dressing room, listening to the clash of the swords, waiting for our call, and talking about the audience. Pam Thompson, who was playing one of the ladies in the banquet scene, always found a way to peek out at the audience, even though Mrs. Mac told us never to do it. Pam said she saw Mrs. Fredericks sitting next to a man who had a mop of dark curly hair. Someone on the other side of the room said she thought Carol Cummings

Oldham, who had played Juliet in the first production, was coming to this show.

I was leaning against the makeup table. Occasionally I saw someone glance over at me with a worried expression and look away quickly. It didn't matter. I was concentrating on playing Juliet.

My first scene was very short. It went without a hitch. But the first kiss came during the banquet scene.

When Zed leaned over and kissed me, I gave a little giggle. A deliberate, bubbly little giggle, totally in character for a young girl getting her first kiss at a party. Everyone onstage tensed when they heard it, but they relaxed when I kissed Romeo back. I was Juliet, in a hopeless freefall into love at first sight.

The audience was with us, laughing, gasping, and groaning at all the right moments. Their reaction fed our performance.

When I said Juliet's most famous line, "Romeo, Romeo! wherefore art thou Romeo," I managed to get enough complaint into the question and in the next lines, so that when I reached, "Tis but thy name that is my enemy," a small sound of "oh" came from the audience. I think it was the first time some people understood the meaning of her words.

When Romeo and I were arguing over whether it was really morning and he had to leave me, our voices were so soft and sweet, no one could doubt we were truly in love.

Sometimes, very rarely, everything in a production works. This was one of those times.

Of course there were little glitches. Once or twice, I forgot a bit of blocking or a line came a little late, but my fellow actors covered for me, and if anyone in the audience noticed, they must have forgiven it instantly. Every time I caught sight of Austin in the wings, he was nodding his approval.

The audience became unusually quiet while I was pleading with my parents not to make me marry Paris. My father, and then my mother, refused to hear me tell them I was already married to Romeo. Finally, I uttered that line of complete desolation that ended the first half of the play:

If all else fail, myself have power to die.

When we heard the waves of applause as the curtain went down for intermission, we knew we had a hit.

People were giving me the thumbs-up sign when I walked into the dressing room, and Pam rushed over to give me a hug.

"Great job," she said, flinging her arms around me.

I felt a splash of liquid land on my arm and heard someone gasp. Pam stepped back, looking in horror from my dress to the open can of grape soda she held in her hand. I glanced down to see purple stains growing down the front and side of my beautiful white brocade costume.

Pam insisted on going with me to the costume shop.

"It was all my fault," Pam said to Mrs. Lester. "I'd smuggled in food for intermission because it's our last opening night."

"We have rules against eating in the theater for a reason," said Mrs. Lester. She glanced up at the monitor. "Everyone must be worried sick. Go tell them Beth will be ready in time. And get that food out of the dressing room before there are any more accidents!"

Mrs. Lester hurried over to a wheeled rack in the middle of the room crammed with costumes in flimsy plastic bags. "Thank goodness the *Cinderella!* costumes just came back from the cleaners," she said as she shuffled through the hangers.

For a moment, I didn't understand why she was searching for my Cat costume. Then I gave a small gasp as I saw her pull out what she'd been looking for.

"We know the gown you wore as the Duchess fits well and the light blue will work for Act Two almost as well as the white."

The blue gown. The unlucky one. The one that jinxed my performance.

This time I had to get out of wearing it.

"But what about the pearls that kept falling off?"

"I took them off as soon as you brought it to me," Mrs. Lester said, holding up the blue dress and peering at it through the tinted plastic. "There's still a jeweled band at the top of the bodice, but that was sewn on separately from the pearls."

I knew she didn't believe that blue dresses were unlucky, but she wouldn't be happy about changing the color of a costume in the middle of a play. The lighting had been set up for white.

"Maybe there's another white gown in the rack room. Wouldn't that be better?"

Mrs. Lester hesitated, then looked up at the monitor again and shook her head. "Intermission's almost over. There isn't time to try on anything else. Better get into this one now."

I had no choice.

I slipped into the costume and glanced down at the decoration, a jeweled band with a flower in its center. I didn't remember it from the last time I wore that dress, but since I'd only worn it once, I hadn't had time to take in much of anything.

I gave the band a tug, just to make sure it wasn't the least bit loose. Then I pulled on the big yellow jewel in the middle for good measure.

I suppose the flower is meant to be a daisy, I thought idly. And then I remembered where I'd seen it before.

"Mrs. Lester," I said very quietly. "Please look at this."

She stood up and looked at the jewels closely.

"That's no costume jewelry," she said, in as quiet a voice as I had used.

Then she laughed and took my hands and squeezed them, grinning at me like the Cheshire Cat. I grinned back at her, even though I doubted finding the bracelet would make a difference.

Mrs. Lester switched her attention to the large stitches holding the bracelet on the dress. "I'll bet the person who sewed that on was no more than nine or ten years old," she said.

"Then I think I know how it got on there," I said slowly. "I put the dress on your repair pile when Mrs. Fredericks was touring the shop. Molly was mending things for you. If Mrs. Fredericks's bracelet fell off her wrist and landed in the mending pile, Molly could have picked it up and sewn it on my costume."

"Molly! I've noticed already that she's got a wonderful sense of design." Mrs. Lester was still grinning.

I tucked my chin down on my collar bone to get a better look. "To think it's been in the theater all along."

Mrs. Lester shook her head. "It wasn't in the theater at all."

I looked at her, confused. "Where was it?"

"After you left, I put that dress in with the dry cleaning and took it all to my car as I went home. Today's the first day it's been back in the shop."

She picked up a pair of scissors from the cutting table, weighed them in her hand, and put them back down. "I can't risk taking the bracelet off now. You've got to be onstage in a perfect costume in two minutes. And the bracelet's as safe there as anywhere else. Go to Mrs. Mac's office immediately after curtain call and she'll clip it off and give it to Mrs. Fredericks."

The diamonds glittered in the light every time I made the smallest move. They were real all right. I had to say something.

"Mrs. Lester, can't you cut it off? Please? It's supposed to be bad luck to wear real jewels onstage."

She looked at me and sighed. "There just isn't time. And you think wearing blue onstage is bad luck, too."

I nodded. "The last time I wore this dress everything went wrong. Tonight's performance is so important . . ." I didn't have to finish the sentence. We both knew what was at stake.

Suddenly Mrs. Lester grinned at me. "I know something I can do to fix it," she said. "I asked some of my friends if they had ever heard blue was unlucky. Between us, we probably have over three hundred years' experience as costumers . . ."

I looked at her expectantly, but she shook her head. "None of them had ever heard anything like that. So I Googled it and I found something on two different websites. They both said that the bad luck will be erased if you wear silver on the blue costume."

She reached over for her pin cushion and took off a string of safety pins. "I can pin these around the bottom of your hem. They'll look like a silver decoration on the gown. What do you think?"

"Won't they show?"

She unclipped the first pin. "Only the people in the first row or two of the audience would be able to see what they were. And if they noticed, they'd just think something went wrong with the hem and I had to pin it up."

I looked at the silver string in her hand. I wanted to have that lucky little row of pins flashing onstage so badly. But this was also Mrs. Lester's opening night, her last one at the theater.

"That's not fair to you," I said. "It would look like you did sloppy work, and you worked so hard on this show."

"I don't mind. Not if it will help you feel more confident onstage." She jiggled the pins in her hand, waiting.

I wavered. It would be so easy to get that little bit of extra luck. And surely I could use some help. I had to go back and show the audience a young girl so in love that she makes desperate, stupid choices and manage to convince them that was how Juliet would act.And then I realized I had all the help I needed. I had Shakespeare's words.

"No, thank you, Mrs. Lester," I said. "I don't need the pins. I'm playing Juliet."

"Break a leg," she whispered as she pointed to the monitor. It was time for me to get back to the stage.

I spent a few minutes alone in the wings. Slowly I cleared my mind of grape soda and diamond bracelets and those words Mrs. Fredericks had spoken. It was time to concentrate on Juliet. When I went onstage, all I was thinking about was Romeo.

Our sad story continued until our parents found us dead in each other's arms. When the curtain came down on our death scene, the audience sat in silence for the longest moment in my life.

Was it that bad? I thought as I scrambled to my feet and hurried offstage for the curtain call.

Then a wave of sound hit me.

Zed and I took our bows last. As we walked out to the front of the stage, holding hands, a stronger wave of sound surged from the audience and I realized everyone was getting to their feet.

"Standing ovation," whispered Zed.

I looked out over the footlights and saw a woman wiping her eyes. But she was standing and clapping and smiling at the same time.

The whole cast was bowing for the third time when there was a disturbance in the fourth row. Mrs. Fredericks was leaving, pushing her way past everyone else. Someone with dark curly hair, who looked a lot like the picture of Quinn Whittaker in the newspaper, followed closely behind her.

That was the moment when I knew we'd lost the theater forever. Mrs. Fredericks had found another theater company to give it to, and she didn't even have the courtesy to stay till the end of our curtain calls.

I looked away and saw both Austin and Scott giving me a thumbs-up from the wings. The rest of the backstage crew had joined in the applause. I smiled quickly at them and then back out at the audience as Zed and I stepped to the front and bowed again. Mrs. Fredericks might take our theater away, but no one could take away what we had just accomplished.

When I looked up, the man with the dark curly hair had turned up the aisle to the lobby, but Mrs. Fredericks had turned in the other direction.

She was climbing the stairs to the stage. She stepped onto it, walked to the exact center, and stood in front of Zed and me.

The audience started to mutter. Hardly anyone knew who she was and no one knew what she was doing, but she held her hand up for silence and got it.

I'll give her the bracelet now, I thought. *Right here, quick. Maybe it could still change her mind.* I reached up to pull it from the dress, but Mrs. Fredericks was already talking.

"As some of you know," she said, "I own this theater. And I plan to turn it into a memorial in honor of my late husband."

A couple of people in the audience started to boo softly, but she held up her hand once more and they stopped. I was picking desperately at the threads that held the bracelet until Mrs. Fredericks went on.

"He loved theater—challenging, memorable plays with great acting—and I can think of no better way to honor his memory than to have his name live on in a theater with an acting company that produced that level of work." Her voice broke when she was talking about honoring his name, just like it had when she told me the daisy bracelet was the last present he had given her.

She took a deep breath. "I finally found that company. Tonight."

The audience was so silent, it seemed like everyone in it was holding their breath. I know all the members of the cast were.

"I plan to give this theater to the city of Oakfield if the city will meet two conditions."

There were a couple of tentative claps but she held her hand up again and continued to speak. "The first condition is that it be renamed the Edward J. Fredericks Memorial Theater. The second is that it remains a children's theater and continues to train the next generation of outstanding actors."

Everyone—the audience, the cast, the crew—burst into applause. Mrs. Fredericks got her own standing ovation.

Zandy, who had heard everything from the lighting booth, shone the spotlight on her.

The spot caught the diamonds on my dress as well. I looked down at the flashes of white and yellow and smiled. I'd just been given a brilliant present. Mrs. Fredericks was going to get one, too.

Epilogue

It is an epilogue or discourse, to make plain
Some obscure precedence that hath tofore been sain.
I will example it

Shakespeare's *Love's Labours Lost*

At the end of some plays, there's an epilogue. An actor just faces the audience and tells them what happened after the last scene. I guess that's the best way to tell you what happened after Mrs. Fredericks gave us the theater for good.

She cried and laughed and cried again when I showed her the bracelet. She's planning on flying in from New York to see every play in the first season of the Edward J. Fredericks Memorial Children's Theater.

Now that the theater is a memorial to her husband, she's become our biggest supporter. She can't do enough for us. She's helped out in the costume shop and started a college scholarship for a theater kid who wants to study drama. She even offered to make tapes of herself speaking so I can work on my New York accent.

Zandy's dad will be flying in, too, as soon as she gets cast in her next play. They talk about it every time he calls, which is a lot more often than he used to.

Romeo and Juliet got a front page write-up in the Oakfield paper. Beside the article, there was a picture of the reporter who wrote it, the curly-haired guy who sat next to Mrs. Fredericks on opening night. He said some very nice things about my acting and my mom pasted the article in a scrapbook she bought just for my reviews.

Guess who played Juliet for the rest of the run?

Emily Chang.

I watched the last performance of *Romeo and Juliet* from the audience. Emily's a better actress than I am. She's been acting almost four years longer. But I'm still working, still studying, still getting better.

Look for me.

I'll be playing Juliet again.

Someday.

THE SHAKESPEARIAN QUOTES

All of the quotes in this book are from William Shakespeare, who is considered one of the greatest writers who ever lived. He was born in England in 1564, during the reign of Queen Elizabeth I, and died in 1616, during the reign of King James I. He was a playwright and a poet and, like Beth, an actor. His writing was very popular and many of his plays, in which he also acted, were produced at the royal palaces.

Almost all the lines that Beth quotes are spoken by Juliet in Shakespeare's play *Romeo and Juliet*. Here are Juliet's lines, the act, and the scene in which they appear in the play, and the page number where you will find them in this book.

JULIET

O, shut the door! and when thou hast done so,
Come weep with me; past hope, past cure, past help!
Romeo and Juliet, Act IV, scene 1.
Pages 138 and 147

Shall I not then be stifled in the vault,
To whose foul mouth no healthsome air breathes in
Romeo and Juliet, Act IV, scene 3.
Pages 139 and 148

Is there no pity sitting in the clouds,
That sees into the bottom of my grief?
O, sweet my mother, cast me not away!
Romeo and Juliet, Act III, scene 5.
Page 139

Hast comforted me marvelous much.
Romeo and Juliet, Act III, scene 5.
Pages 140 and 148

Romeo, I come! this do I drink to thee.
Romeo and Juliet, Act IV, scene 3.
Page 154

O Romeo, Romeo! wherefore art thou Romeo?
Tis but thy name that is my enemy
Romeo and Juliet, Act II, scene 2.
Pages 137, 160, and 175

If all else fail, myself have power to die
Romeo and Juliet, Act III, scene 5.
Pages 163 and 176

The Epigraphs

An epigraph is a quote that appears at the beginning of a chapter or a book. It usually echoes or foretells an idea or event in the writing that follows.

All but one of the epigraphs that appear in this book are taken from Shakespeare's plays. One epigraph is from a poem he wrote. You can tell which one is a poem because the title is written within quotation marks instead of being italicized.

Prologue
Page 3:

The actors are at hand and by their show
You shall know all that you are like to know.
Quince, *A Midsummer Night's Dream*, Act V, scene 1

Chapter One
Page 7:

Pins and poking-sticks of steel,
What maids lack from head to heel:
Autolycus, **The Winter's Tale,** Act IV, scene 4

Chapter Two
Page 15:

. . . here is that
which will give language to you, cat: open
your mouth; this will shake your shaking,
Stephano, **The Tempest,** Act II, scene 2

Chapter Three
Page 29:

now must we to her window,
And give some evening music to her ear.
Proteus, **Two Gentlemen of Verona,** Act IV, scene 2

Chapter Four
Page 41:

Wilt thou spit all thyself?
Pericles, **Pericles,** Act II, scene 1

Chapter Five
Page 53:

What think you of a duchess? have you limbs
To bear that load of title?
Old Lady, **Henry VIII, Act II, scene 3**

Chapter Six
Page 69:

And all the secrets of our camp I'll show,
Their force, their purposes; nay, I'll speak that
Which you will wonder at.
Parolles, **All's Well that Ends Well, Act IV, scene 1**

Chapter Seven
Page 83:

We two alone will sing like birds i' th' cage.
Lear, **King Lear, Act V, scene 3**

Chapter Eight
Page 93:

Search for a jewel that too casually
Hath left mine arm:
Imogen, **Cymbeline, Act II, scene 3**

Chapter Nine
Page 107:

Then how or which way should they first break in?
Question, my lords, no further of the case,
How or which way: 'tis sure they found some place
But weakly guarded, where the breach was made.
King Charles and La Pucelle, **Henry VI, Part 1, Act II, scene 1**

Chapter Ten
Page 119:

When sorrows come, they come not single spies but in battalions!
Claudius, **Hamlet, Act IV, scene 5**

Chapter Eleven
Page 135:

Read on this book,
That show of such an exercise may colour
Your loneliness.
Polonius, **Hamlet, Act III, scene 1**

Chapter Twelve
Page 151:

Like a dull actor now, I have forgot my part,
Coriolanus, **Coriolanus, Act V, scene 3**

Chapter Thirteen
Page 163:

But when her lips were ready for his pay,
He winks, and turns his lips another way.
"Venus and Adonis," line 105

Chapter Fourteen
Page 173:

I pray you mar no more of my verses with reading them
ill-favouredly.
Orlando, *As You Like It*, Act III, scene 2

Epilogue
Page 187:

it is an epilogue or discourse, to make plain
Some obscure precedence that hath tofore been sain.
I will example it:
Don Adriano de Armado, **Love's Labours Lost**, Act III, scene 1

THE SCOTTISH PLAY

For hundreds of years, actors have been superstitious about saying the name of the Scottish play. No one knows why this play got a reputation for being cursed. Some blame Shakespeare for including three witches in the play. They think he quoted the spells of real witches when he wrote their lines.

The only exception to this rule is when the Scottish play is being produced onstage. But even appearing in it is considered unlucky. There are countless stories about falling scenery, lopped off thumbs, riots, heart attacks, car accidents, and even deaths that have occurred during the run of this play.

Those who don't believe in the curse argue that because much of the play is set at night, the darkness of the set—combined with all the knives, sword fights, and battles called for in the script—increases the possibility of injuries.

Most actors don't buy it, and I'm not going to jinx this book by writing the name of the play here. If you haven't figured it out yet, Zandy has. You can read her solution on page 52.

Beth's quote from the Scottish play:

By the pricking of my thumbs,
Something wicked this way comes
Second Witch, **Shakespeare's Scottish play, Act IV, scene 1,** pages 3, 13, 18, 24, 42, and 74

Acknowledgments

This book started when my aunts, Dorothy Smith and Eileen Boitel, took me to my first Broadway play and introduced me to the wonder of theater. I have never forgotten that production of *Peter Pan*.

I learned much of what I know about the work involved in putting on a play from the production of *Just So Stories* that Patricia Briggs adapted and staged at the Palo Alto Children's Theatre. Caryn Huberman Yacowitz and I photographed the show and wrote the photo essay *Onstage/Backstage* about it. Pat and the children in the cast and crew were so generous and cooperative as we worked around them. They made us feel welcome in their theater.

There are many similarities between my fictional Oakfield Children's Theater and the Palo Alto Children's Theatre, though I have changed its practices, the layout of the building, and the history of its founding to suit the purposes of this book. The Palo Alto Children's Theatre, which opened in 1937, was built on a city park and given to the city of Palo Alto, California, by a generous local philanthropist, Lucie Stern. She has the gratitude of the thousands of children who have taken part in the theatre over the years, as well as of the thousands of adults like me who have enjoyed its productions. Three directors have led the theater over most of the last eighty years: Hazel Glaister Robertson, Patricia Briggs, and, most recently, Judge Luckey. None of them is a model for Mrs. Mac, but they all share a love of theater and an understanding of how to nurture and support the children who act or who are members of the crew. I owe a special debt to Alison Williams, the Palo Alto Children's Theatre's costume supervisor for the last thirty years, for sharing her knowledge of designing and building costumes and for helping me research the question of wearing blue onstage.

Jane Yolen, the award-winning author of more than three hundred books, read the earliest draft of this manuscript at a writer's workshop she taught, and her advice shaped every rewrite I did. Caryn Huberman Yacowitz is a member of both of my critique groups. She and Karen Beaumont, Dayle Ann Dodds, Betsy Franco, Emily Jiang, Ann Manheimer, Marjorie Sayer, and the late Angela Haight contributed so much to improving *Playing Juliet*. An invaluable help was my daughter, Jillian Wetzel Stirling, who shared her experience as an actor both at the Palo

Alto Children's Theatre and also with professional theater groups. I am embarrassed to remember how many early drafts I asked her to read and how many errors she caught.

I am grateful for the encouragement of all the people who volunteered to read an early copy of this manuscript, including Lisa Hodges, Molly Riley, and Scott Stirling, who were then in middle school, and to children's librarians Jan Pedden and Claudia Davis.

My agent, Sara Sciuto, believed in this book and found the perfect editor for my manuscript, Julie Matysik, who is as big a Shakespeare fan as I am. Her assistant, Adrienne Szpyrka, made some important contributions to the plot. Thanks to you all.

And, as always, a very special thank-you to my husband, Gary, for his constant support and continued applause.

About the Author

JoAnne Stewart Wetzel saw her first play, *Peter Pan*, on Broadway when she was seven years old. There were pirates and Indians, a fairy, and the actors flew! Ever since, she's known something magical might happen at any moment in a theater. That's one reason she's seen a production of every play written by William Shakespeare. Her first book, *Onstage/Backstage*, which she wrote and illustrated with Caryn Huberman Yacowitz, was a photo essay about putting on a play at the Palo Alto Children's Theatre. She and her husband live in the San Francisco Bay area. They have one daughter, who started acting at their local children's theater when she was nine. To find out more about JoAnne and the book, please visit her website at www.joannewetzel.com.